THE MAN
WHO WOULD BE
GOD

SOUTHWEST

LIFE AND LETTERS

A series designed to publish
outstanding new fiction and
nonfiction about Texas and the
American Southwest and to
present classic works of the region
in handsome new editions.

GENERAL EDITORS: Kathryn Lang,
Southern Methodist University Press;
Tom Pilkington, *Tarleton State
University.*

The
MAN Who
Would Be
GOD

Stories by

PAUL RUFFIN

Southern Methodist University Press
DALLAS

These stories are works of fiction. Names, characters, places, and in-
cidents are either the product of the author's imagination or are used
fictitiously. Any resemblance to actual events, locales, or persons, living or dead, is entirely coincidental.

Copyright © 1993 by Paul Ruffin
All rights reserved
Printed in the United States of America

FIRST EDITION, 1993

Requests for permission to reproduce material from this work should be sent to:
    Permissions
    Southern Methodist University Press
    Box 415
    Dallas, Texas 75275

Some of the stories in this collection first appeared in the following
publications: "The Fox" in *Ploughshares;* "Grief" (as "The Grave") in
American Literary Review; "The Man Who Would Be God" in *Chari-
ton Review;* "The Return" in *Kansas Quarterly;* and "Storm" in *American Way.*

Library of Congress Cataloging-in-Publication Data
Ruffin, Paul.
    The man who would be God : stories / Paul Ruffin. — 1st ed.
      p.   cm. — (Southwest life and letters)
    Contents: The fox — The beast within — Storm — The deputy —
The return — The survivalist — Grief — Eleanor's caller — The
hunt — Lamar Loper's first case — The man who would be God.
    ISBN 0-87074-354-6. — ISBN 0-87074-363-5 (pbk.)
    I. Title. II. Series.
PS3568.U362M36   1993
813'.54—dc20   93-5225

Cover art and design by Barbara Whitehead

For Sharon

CONTENTS

THE

FOX

FROM where she was sitting at the kitchen table, her hands deep in the ball of dough in a green bowl, she could see him cross the creek beyond the lower pasture and angle up toward the house. He stopped to lean on the fence that bordered the remains of the summer garden, where the bean poles still stood at odd angles beside the all-but-leafless okra stalks. Drought had brought the garden to an early end as it almost always did.

She was dumping the dough out onto the counter when his shadow mounted the steps and filled the doorway. The screen door squawked open, then slammed to behind him. She did not look around.

"There was a fox," he said, sliding a chair back from the table and sitting down, "a red one, in the back field. Near the low-water crossing." He leaned and lifted the coffeepot from the counter and filled the cup that he had already emptied twice that morning before leaving the house. The sun, still morning low, slanted into the small kitchen, brightening what inexpensive things she had scattered across it on table and counter and walls over the thirteen years that they had lived there. Dust specks spun in the rays.

"He had one leg hanging silly to the side and dragging and leaving blood." He looked to see whether she had heard. She kept shaping the ball of dough. "He was so close I could see his eyes. I swear they looked like, like he was blaming me for what trouble he'd been in." He reached over and slid open the box of matches by the stove, one-handedly, lifted one out and struck it across the tabletop and lit a cigarette. Blue smoke curled up and ribboned in the sun.

She dusted her hands with flour and flattened out the dough, rolled it, and lifted the sheet over a pie plate and dropped it into place. With a paring knife she sliced off the excess, leaving a neat edge around the rim of the plate.

"What you making?" he asked.

"Pie."

"What kind? Something special?"

"No. Just a blueberry pie, from them berries I picked back earlier and froze." She stirred the berries again for good measure and lifted them from the burner.

"His eyes. I can't get over his eyes. They looked like cracked marbles, only black and cold. I was almost afraid he was going to come after me, he looked so mad at the world."

She poured the berries into the dough-lined plate and patted them level with her hand with short little strokes to avoid burning herself, then dropped another sheet of dough over the top. Her hands were stained a deep purple. Using the tines of a fork, she crimped the top shell onto the bottom and ran the knife around the rim again, leaving the pie picture-perfect and ready for baking. She struck three vent slits in the top and slid it into the oven.

"One of them old coon traps likely." He looked at her. "I guess that's what he got into. Hell, I ain't checked them things in years. I left maybe four, five right near where he was."

She dried her berry-stained hands on her apron front, walked to the back door, and looked off toward the smoky morning woods. Crows were zipping in and out of a tree by the creek, cawing, diving in, wheeling up and out, cawing and diving in again. "Owl," she said quietly, "they must be after an owl or something."

"What?" He turned toward her.

"Nothing. I was just talking out loud to myself." She returned to the table and sat down across from him, not because she wanted particularly to be there but because there was no place she could get off to in such a small house where his voice would not find her, rising in insistence until she came. She was not certain that he even cared whether she listened or not. She was just another living thing his voice could drive into or bounce off of— she was something to keep him from talking to himself, which even he must have known was proof positive that he had crossed over into craziness.

"He must have got into one last night, broke his foot or leg, could have gnawed it off to get out, though I couldn't see the tip of it to be sure." He squinted as smoke coiled about his face. "He crawled under the fence and got off into Mason's corn, what there is of it, not much more than enough to hide a fox, I'd say. Could have been the one that killed them chickens last month, same size, same color. Not likely to get at'm again."

Their relationship, from her intense hatred of him when they were in grade school together through an infatuation in high school that was consummated in her father's hayloft one Sunday afternoon, had come finally full circle, back to something that she thought at times was hate, at other times mere indifference. If she wished him harm, as she found herself doing some days when he was off in the fields and she was alone in the little house or out in the garden, she was almost happy to see, once he appeared at the door, that none had come to him. Those times the hate swung much too quickly to something like love.

It was the indifference that she nurtured, the cold distance that she put between herself and him even when he was close enough that she could see the hardness of his eyes. It was the calm deadness of indifference that allowed her to continue, day after day, to endure the hill and house and his voice and, each night that he rose to it, to accept his heavy roughness as he drove into her until he shuddered and rolled off onto his side of the bed.

"You shoulda seen them eyes. Like he was blaming me."

3

She stared past him, past the dust specks in the beam of sun that crossed his face, past the dreamlike haziness of the screen, to the wall of woods where the crows were still zipping in and out of the tree where she was sure some owl crouched, or hawk, something wiser or nobler than crows.

"May die from it, may not. Lucky he didn't die in the trap. He's got something to be glad of there."

And there were the times she was sure that she wished him dead, gone, so that she could try to find some value again in her life, some meaning, before she was stooped and gray and broken like her mother until a merciful onslaught of pneumonia took her out of it, leaving her father so alone that even he, in all his hardness, lasted only another year. She was not so old now—though you could not tell it looking at her hands and face, where the wind and sun and contact with all the things that sting and slash and burn on a farm had done their damage—that she could not smooth over and grow graceful, as her mother had wanted, had taught her to be. She did not even have a child to pass her dreams on to, no matter what their possibilities or impossibilities. She was not certain that his savage seed, which burned in her like a burst of flame, could beget anything softer than a boy, who would be a copy of him.

"I guess I ought to get the shotgun and go finish him off," he said after several minutes, "if he ain't got too far by now." He flicked his cigarette toward the ashtray and dropped the butt into the last of his coffee. It extinguished with a short hiss.

She walked over to the oven, swung the door down, and checked on the pie. The smell billowed up and out and filled the kitchen.

He slid his chair back and walked into their bedroom, where she heard him fumbling in the closet, getting his gun and shells. He emerged, broke the shotgun open, slipped in two red shells, and stood there watching her bent over the pie. "I don't know how long I'll be gone."

She straightened. The sun had crept along the floor now until the corridor of light from the door was only half as long as it had been. Its reflection off the linoleum gave his face an almost blessed look, like that of the saints in pictures she had seen, but his eyes were still dark and merciless, and the hard lines in his face stood out. He smiled and reached to touch her hand where it lay on the counter. She pulled it away.

"You . . . ," he began, then dropped his head and turned to the door to go.

Watching out of the corner of her eye as his shadow darkened the doorway, paused, and disappeared, she took the pie out of the oven and set it onto a back burner. The house quieted then, dropped so far into silence that she could hear nothing but wind stirring the okra stalks and the distant chatter of crows. She walked to the screen and saw him blend into the woods. A tight smile on her face, she looked once around the little kitchen and walked over to the stove, where she poised her hand at the edge of the pie and plunged it into the hot, dark center, where it stayed until the burning stopped and there was no feeling left at all.

THE
BEAST
WITHIN

"Is there anybody with you?" The voice was low and raspy, only vaguely female, like that of a woman hardened into her late years from loss and longing or abuse at the hands of a sorry man. In the dying afternoon I could only guess at what she looked like—the door was cracked the distance a safety chain would allow and there was no light on behind her.

"My wife." I nodded toward the car, settled like a crippled beast on its left front, where the absurd little temporary spare just barely held the bumper off the ground.

"Tell her to get out and come on up."

"Well, she's pretty tired and disgusted with things. All I want—"

The voice came back harsh: "She don't get out, you don't get in. Ain't no man coming in here without his woman is with him. Tell her to come on." The door had not moved.

"Annie, come on. It's OK." I motioned for her to join me. She slid across and got out on my side, leaving the door open, then leaned back in and yanked her purse to her. Taking care to avoid the deep erosion channel that cut across the driveway and looking around to be certain that there were no dogs about, she finally came up beside me. "Jesus," I heard her mumble.

"Now," the voice said just as a light blazed on above my head and another came on at each corner of the building, trapping us in a cross-fire of brilliance, "lace your fingers together, both of you, and put your hands on top of your heads. Then get on your knees."

"Ma'am?" I started, glancing to the side at my wife, who was squinting at me.

"Boy, if you two ain't on your knees time I count three, you are dead. You look at what's sticking through this door and you'll see it's the barrel of a .44 magnum. Now, down!"

On a short late-summer vacation, the last trip before my university teaching started again at Memphis State, my wife and I were traveling from Memphis to Houston to visit relatives, trying to make the trip in a day. Late that Thursday afternoon we had stopped at a truck stop just north of Lufkin, Texas, and gassed up, ready for the last leg of the journey, when I asked one of the attendants at the pumps how long it would take us to get to Houston.

"Well," he drawled, spitting a stain of brown onto the concrete, "ordinarily it wouldn't take you very long at all, but since them heavy rains earlier this week—" He pointed across the apron to a red gash where apparently a ramp had exited onto the interstate; a barricade made of barrels and timbers blocked it off. "Nearly washed us away. Like I was saying, if them rains hadn't come, it wouldn't take you no time to get down there, but they was doing some work on the highway at the time and all that got washed out, so now they got the regular repair work plus having to redo what they had already got done."

"So you're saying that they're working on the highway?" my wife leaned across and asked. She was holding the map that we had been using. She was not enjoying the trip.

"Yes'm, that's what I'm saying. Working right into the night, right up until it gets so dark that they have to quit. So if you don't want to get jammed up down there in all that mess, you better go a back way."

I took the map from my wife and held it out to him. "Would you show us a good way to go that will get us past the road work?"

"Yeah, but I don't need that. There's a real good back way if you ain't got to get gas, which you ain't, between here and there—ain't no gas stations in there at all, maybe a couple of old stores." He reached over and began drawing a crude map in the grime of the hood, thumping out landmarks along a tortuous finger-line of road and announcing them like a tour guide. When he was finished, he looked in at us. "Got it?" We nodded. "It's the easiest way, and besides, you'll get a better idea of what East Texas is like than you would going on in on the big highway. More to see."

I thanked him and drove off, watching closely for the exit just south of town that would mark the beginning of the map on the hood.

"Bobby, I think we ought to stick with the main highway." She rarely went along with any decision I made.

"No, let's try this. We've got a full tank of gas and plenty of sun left. We've never seen much of East Texas—you don't learn anything about a place from traveling along its interstates." I folded the map and handed it to her to put away. Her long blond hair fell across her shoulders and blazed in the sun as she slid the map under her seat. Then we entered the shadows of the trees.

The road was not a bad one, albeit it was narrow and winding, and trees—this was part of the wilderness area known as the Big Thicket—came right up to the shoulders. It was trash-strewn, as most rural roads are in areas populated by low-income families, and the presence of paper and plastic at a uniform height in the undergrowth suggested that it had been recently flooded. We encountered no traffic except occasional home-bound log trucks, their trailers empty and banging along like playthings, which we nervously squeezed past.

What we struck with the left front tire—I saw it at an appreciable distance, saw it but could not for the life of me avert the

car from that certain collision, drawn inexorably toward it, mesmerized—was a metal bracket that probably had bounced off one
of the trucks. The treads caught one leg of the bracket and
flipped the other leg up, driving its tapered edge through the
outer wall of the tire. Blowout! Much swerving and squealing of
rubber and we came to rest finally with half the car on asphalt,
the other half on the narrow gravel shoulder that separated the
road from dark, towering trees.

My wife sat in awful silence as I shifted luggage around and
freed the jack and spare, one of those silly little temporaries made
to get you by for a few miles and save Detroit money. The bracket
had gashed the tire beyond repair; I held it up for Annie to see
before throwing it into the trunk.

"Oh, wonderful. How long can we go on that little donut you
put on?" She did not bother to disguise her mood.

"I don't know. A few miles." She looked so helpless and out-of-
place in her delicate checked blouse and designer jeans against
the backdrop of heavy woods. I smiled at her. "Maybe there's a
station up ahead."

She looked out at the wall of trees as I started the engine.
"Don't you remember what he said? There are no service stations
on this road."

"Well, maybe, Goddamn it," I snapped, "he's wrong. Besides,
he did mention that there were a couple of stores."

"Yeah, but maybe, Goddamn it, he's wrong."

"Can we please pull together this time? Just this once?"

"Bobby, I cannot tell you how I hate this, how I hate *everything*
we do together!" Her fists were clenched at her sides.

Easing the car onto the road, I accelerated until I had reached
a speed that I decided the tire could endure without ripping
apart. We were tilted down on the left front. "It's like we're in a
perpetual hole," my wife said, nervously watching the road and
turning from time to time to stare out at the towering trees on
each side. Concerned that yet another bracket or beer bottle lay
in our path, I kept my eyes on the road ahead, glancing aside only
when the trees thinned or a logging road broke the impenetrable
green curtain. There were no signs, nothing but trees.

We passed neither store, house, nor mailbox, not another truck or car from either direction for agonizingly long miles as the road led us, deeper and darker, to the south. Then, just as my wife slid down in her seat and closed her eyes to await that bang on the left front that would stop us, trap us there, perhaps all night, on that darkening road, just as I had all but given up hope of finding any vestige of civilization again, the opening came. Around an abrupt curve, at the top of a steep incline, it sat at the edge of a semicircle of gravel: an old concrete-block store building, white at one time, with a barely discernible name, AUTRY'S GRO-CERY, flanked by RC Cola signs.

A sagging tin-covered garage with rusty grease-rack sat next to the building, and halfway between the two stood an old gas pump, hoseless, like an unarmed sentinel against the coming night. Behind the buildings and to the sides the land, cleared apparently for farming, fell away sharply to the dark woods.

"Look." I tapped my wife's leg as I eased over onto the shoulder and stopped, taking care to avoid the deep channel, cut by recent rains, that ran like a moat across the gravel drive and isolated the store from the road.

She sat up, blinking. "It worked. Bobby, it worked! I closed my eyes and told myself that when I opened them it would be like coming out of a bad dream."

"Well, judging from the erosion here and the weeds all over the place, this might not be the oasis you were hoping to wake up to. But at least," I said confidently, pulling the car onto the shoulder as far as I could without dropping into the cut, "at least it's a place where we can get off the road and maybe stay the night and phone for help or flag someone down in the morning."

I sat for a minute or two studying the building, looking for signs of life. There were curtains covering the windows on each side of the front door, but as late as it was, there should have been lights if anyone were home. The bed of a pickup protruded from behind the garage, but it was canted up oddly as if it rested on blocks, doubtless abandoned.

"Well, I don't see anyone, no dogs, no lights, nothing, so I guess I'll go check it out. You just stay in the car." When I opened the door to get out, she looked so small and delicate, her feet folded up beneath her on the seat, that I reached over and squeezed her hand. "Everything's going to be all right, Annie. I'll be right back."

"All right, boy—using one hand at a time, empty your pockets out on the ground, and do it real slow, like syrup at Christmas. Remember that this .44 makes a hole smaller than a dime going in, but it'll take off the back of your skull on the way out."

With dream-like slowness I removed the car keys and change from my pants pocket, laid them in the gravel before me, then my billfold and handkerchief. My wife, somewhere just behind to my left, had dropped her purse beside me on the way to her knees. The muzzle of the .44 inched through the door and pointed to it.

"If that's all you got in your pockets, and it better be all, dump the purse and scatter the stuff out."

I reached and got the purse, unzipped it, and emptied its contents in an arc between me and the door: lipstick, keys, compact, coin purse, checkbook, credit-card folder, fingernail file, pens, a packet of tissues, all the odds and ends a woman does not feel comfortable without. How absurdly useless they looked spread out in the gravel, those trappings of another world.

"Ma'am." I looked at the barrel fixed on me. "We're not armed, I assure you. This is all we're carrying."

Silence. Long, unearthly silence. I could hear the shallow, fast breathing of my wife, sounds of night birds in the darkening woods, and in my temples the heavy throb of my heart, like a distant war drum.

"OK, just leave that stuff on the ground and come in here, on all fours, slow, *real* slow."

I looked up at the door as it closed slightly, the safety chain rattled, and the door swung open. "You mean," I asked the dark doorway, she apparently having backed into the depths of the room, "you want us to crawl in there? Like animals?" No answer came back. I turned and looked at my wife, whose hair had fallen over her face so that I could not see her eyes, and crawled slowly into the dark room.

When I reached what seemed to be the center, I felt Annie touch one of my feet and stopped. What were we to do then, powerless on our hands and knees in a dark store building in the middle of nowhere with a .44 magnum aimed at us by an old woman who, from all I could judge, was mad as the wind? I could hear only the shallow panting of my wife and—could it be the old woman?—the rapid breathing of another creature.

"Lady," I said finally, exasperated by the silence and dark, "would you please turn on a light and let us get up? We're not here to do you any harm."

The voice came back dry and hard and uncomfortably close to my right ear. "You just stay on all fours when I turn it on. I'll have this gun on you. And Duke will be watching."

Then the light came on, at first so intensely bright that I had to close my eyes and gradually open them to the details of the room. The old woman, maybe sixty, maybe over seventy, so punished by whatever forces had dogged her life that her face looked like weathered stone as it stared coldly past the sight of the .44, squatted at an inner doorway; her left hand slid down the wall from the light switch. Beside her, his eyes fixed on mine, crouched an enormous black and silver German shepherd.

"Well, sir, they don't look all that dangerous now, do they, Duke?" She patted the dog's head. "You can set up, if you want to, but stay where you're at."

I sat back on my legs and looked at my wife, whose face was so contorted by fear, by the uncertainty of the past few minutes, that I believe I would not have recognized it on a street somewhere. She fell forward into my arms and sobbed; her thin shoulders heaved and shuddered as I stroked her hair. "It's OK, Baby, it's OK."

We were in a large room, what once had obviously been the main part of the store. Old Coca-Cola coolers, brushed over with white paint, lined one wall, and above them hung calendars and cardboard advertisements of products that could not have been sold there in over thirty years. Cheap furniture, bearing the scars of years of use and obvious marring by a large animal allowed to roam freely and sprawl where he wished, was scattered across the room, and simple board shelves, anchored to the concrete block walls with angle-iron braces, were spaced out over the wall opposite the Coca-Cola coolers. Crude pottery—made perhaps by her?—dotted the shelves, along with a variety of cheap vases, depression glass, and old soft drink bottles and oil cans, many of them whose shapes and labels I did not recognize. A hubcap collection hung on either side of the front door.

"You about through looking the place over?" She still had the gun, enormous in her small hand, leveled at my face, the hammer back, her finger across the trigger; I could see the gray bullet heads in the cylinder.

"Ma'am, would you please put the gun down? We can't do you any harm." Behind me my wife, trembling and making small gasps that, I swear, sounded like someone swept up in the raptures of lovemaking, clutched my shirt with both hands.

"You can't be too sure these days." She eased the barrel down until it pointed at my knees. "There's too much meanness going on. Back before I take'n to defending myself properly, back when my daddy was alive and run the store, we was robbed a couple of times a year by thugs up from Houston. They even beat him up a few times until he put a sawed-off shotgun under the counter. After he killed a couple of niggers, people started letting him alone. Folks let me alone too."

"Yes'm, I'm sure of it."

She slid down onto the floor and leaned against the wall, one hand on the dog, the other resting the .44 across her leg. "I am what people call a survivalist," she said, baring her teeth, what few were left. "I got a arsenal here: pistols and shotguns and two high-power rifles, with more ammunition for all of them than you could count in two days. Got bob-wire strung so thick around the back side of the place, down along the woods, that a snake couldn't get through without tearing hisself up."

"Could we get up off the floor?" My wife still trembled at my back.

"No sir. You stay where you are at. What I can't control is people coming in off the road. The county won't let me string bob-wire along the road, so people could stop right out front and attack the place without me having time to get a gun on'm. I got to wait until I got the advantage, the way I do on you now. And I ain't going to take no chances on losing that advantage."

"But, lady, we are a couple in trouble. We need a tire, we need to use your phone. We have people in Houston expecting us early this evening."

"I ain't got tires—this ain't even a store anymore. I've done retired from the store business. And I don't have no phone."

My wife leaned past me and asked in a thin, childlike voice, "You don't have a *telephone?*"

"Naw, missy, I don't. I ain't got nobody to call, and I don't want nobody calling me. I just want to be left alone." She waved the gun around the room. "This is my kingdom and my castle, and I got the right to defend it."

"But lady, we are no threat to you." Ignoring the pistol, I stood and pulled my wife to her feet. "We'll just go back through that door and leave you to your castle and your kingdom."

I heard the hammer click back—I didn't even notice that she had let it down. The dog rumbled low in his throat. "You get back on that floor if you want to live to leave when I decide to let you leave." The .44 was aimed at my face again. "Once you get in, you don't get out until I say so."

"Oh, my God," my wife whimpered, crumpling to the floor. I dropped down beside her.

"You ain't going nowhere till morning." This time I saw her ease the hammer down, one-handed, the pistol as familiar to her as a frying pan. She kept it pointed in our general direction.

"Please, lady," my wife said quietly, "just let us leave. We will get into our car and drive off and we can all pretend that this never happened."

"No, little lady, you are my guests for the night." She pushed the dog to the side and motioned for us to follow her. "I expect that you're hungry, so I'm going to open the kitchen back up and get you fed. What you want?"

My wife and I looked at each other. Five years married, most of it a shaky tenure at best, we did not often look long into each other's eyes, perhaps because neither of us suspected that we would find much truth there, even if we dared to look. She had her work, I mine, and we were seldom home together, for one year-long stretch even living across town from each other, she in our old apartment, I in a tiny efficiency near the university. I'd suspected her of having affairs, and she had suspected me, but neither of us had cared enough to bring the matter up since early on in the marriage. She had never really told me what she saw in me that brought us together, and I had not dared to tell her that but for a finely sculpted body, I found little in her attractive. It had been a cold, passionless marriage, characterized by a strained courtesy for the most part, a marriage of convenience, devoid of any real emotional involvement and shared interests. When we made our occasional love, it was quick, almost mechanical, almost like not making love at all. She once said to me, "Other couples make love to each other. All we do is screw, and you are the one who does the screwing—I'm just your legal whore."

Enhanced by fear and the tenuous light of the room, her eyes were an unbelievable pale blue, a fact that I had forgotten. I stared into them and they into me until the old woman slammed the kitchen door back against the wall and told us to come and sit down at the table. I stood and pulled Annie to her feet. We settled into our chairs across from each other, our eyes coming together again, as if we had discovered something for the first time, something deliciously forbidden and sensual.

Laying the .44 onto the counter beside her, the old woman leaned back and pointed to cabinets lining the walls. "Now, I got all kinds of canned meat and stuff, and jars of beans and okry and just about any veg'table you can name, rice, flour, salt meat—you name it and I got it. You remember that I'm a survivalist. I got food here to last me two years, probably, without having to go out for anything. What y'all want t'eat?"

We continued to stare at each other. "Can you eat anything?" I asked her. She had thrust her feet between my feet.

"Yes. I don't know why, but I'm hungry."

I looked at the old woman. "What can you fix that will be quick?"

"What about egg sandwiches? And co-colas?"

"Fine," my wife and I said in unison. I looked into her eyes again. "I didn't know you liked egg sandwiches."

"Never had one." She smiled. "Why not live dangerously?"

We sat at the table staring at each other while the old woman busied herself at the stove frying eggs, smearing mayonnaise on the bread, slicing tomatoes, all the while carrying on a rambling monologue about her castle against a wicked world, how one day the rockets would rain down on America and destroy all but those who were prepared for Armageddon. "Just people like me will be left to carry on, people that's got the sense to be ready, that can defend theirselves against the rest of the world." She brandished the mayonnaise knife against a shadowy enemy that hovered somewhere behind the concrete-block walls.

"You figure the Russians will attack you, huh?" I asked, relieved. In the rich smell of frying eggs she seemed like someone's grandmother in any kitchen, the only thing incongruous the .44 lying among plates and forks and spatulas. I felt almost like teasing her, the way I did my mother about religion. "When do you suppose they'll come?"

"Oh, it ain't the Russians I worry about. It's the beast within that worries me. When the time comes, I'll be blazing away at all them starving people, the niggers and meskins and white trash up from Houston that'll be trying to take this place."

Annie grinned at me. She was lightly rubbing her feet against my legs. "Why would they want to come here?"

The old woman slid saucers with egg sandwiches before us. "To get my food and guns is why. They'll come here to take all the stuff I've stored up. To get my tractor and the gas I got, my two cows and the goats down there." She motioned toward the woods behind the building. "It'll be all them have-nots trying to take from the got-mores. Oh, it ain't the Russians I worry about at all. They'll shoot their rockets and we'll shoot ours and that'll be all we'll ever hear about them again. But what's left over here, the beast within, is what we got to worry about." She turned and began washing the skillet and utensils, her hands moving over and around the pistol as if it were merely another kitchen tool.

After we had eaten and finished our Cokes, the old woman sat down at the table with us, leaving the pistol on the counter. At last I could really study her face: the heavily wrinkled forehead and eyes and cheeks, the poorly kept teeth, the wattled neck. She looked back and forth at us as she talked of her long isolation there in the store building, the death of her father after three years of coma, her mother's death two decades before that, her childhood as daughter of a small farmer and store owner, where her family had come from. My wife and I listened politely, looking at each other from time to time, at times losing ourselves in each other's eyes.

Finally the rambling story of her life ended and she pointed across the hallway to a door. "I'm gon' put y'all in the old store-room for the night. There's a mattress rolled up in there that you can throw out for a pallet. I'll get you some sheets. In the morning you can flag somebody down on the road and hitch a ride to a phone."

We stood at that and I reached across and took my wife's hand. "Could we go to the car and get some things for the night?"

"Naw." The old woman shook her head. "I'm coming to like you and trust you, but I ain't taking no chances. Naw, you done been fed, so now you got to go to bed." She motioned us toward a door. "There's the bathroom. I'll set right here while y'all use it, one at a time. Be quick about it. Then you got to go to bed. It's well after dark."

I motioned for Annie to go on to the bathroom while I sat at the table with the old woman, who had retrieved the .44 from the counter.

"Now, Duke sleeps in that hallway most of the time, except when he's in bed with me, and he sleeps light. If he hears any noise much, he's just as likely to bust that door down as not and tear y'all up. I sleep light too, and I don't ask no questions in the dark. You come out of that room, Duke or me one will get you. You stay in that room and you be quiet and things will be fine. Come morning you can go anywhere you want to."

After my turn in the bathroom, Annie and I entered the hot, musty storeroom, feeling around in the dark for a light switch, stumbling over crates of jars and cans. "Where's the light?" I finally yelled at the old woman through the closed door.

"There ain't one," she yelled back. The door opened briefly and she slid in a bundle of something. "Here's you some sheets. You won't need nothing heavier."

I leaned my face to the door. "Is there a fan or anything in here? It's hot."

"No, there ain't no fan in there." She was still standing at the door. "That's a storeroom. Don't need a fan in there." After a few seconds she said, "It'll cool down d'rectly. That's just the heat from the sun still in them blocks. It'll get better. Now, go t'sleep."

I reached for my wife and pulled her down next to me on one of the crates. We sat in silence a few minutes, waiting for our eyes to become accustomed enough to the dark to make out something of the physical layout of the room. A small barred, glassless window high up on the outer wall admitted the faintest glow of the sky. We could see stars—there was no moon.

"It's like a small prison," she whispered finally. "Concrete, bars, guards, a mattress to sleep on. It's like we're in some kind of foreign country, like we're in a movie."

"Yeah," I whispered back.

"I have never been as scared as I have been tonight. I feel almost like another person." She was gripping my hand. "Have you ever been as scared?"

"No. This has been one awful night for me, and I don't know that it's going to get any better." I pulled her close to me. "I guess we ought to find the mattress and spread our sheets out and try to sleep. Who knows what kind of mood she'll be in in the morning. She might decide during the night to execute us at dawn."

Groping around the walls of the room we found a doubled-up narrow mattress in a corner, quietly slid the crates out to make space, and unrolled it onto the floor. The sheets were, I noticed gratefully, fresh-smelling, as if they had been dried in the sun. When we had the bottom sheet stretched out and tucked under the corners of the mattress, the other folded back at one end for cover, I asked her whether she thought we ought to undress or not.

"What do you think? It's awfully hot in here."

"I don't know," I whispered. "I'm almost afraid to take even my shoes off. Hell, I don't know what to do. Can't brush our teeth or take a bath or anything." I lay back on the mattress and stared up at the dark ceiling.

She eased down beside me, hooking a hand in mine. We lay in silence for a long time, staring up at the ceiling and the barred window. All noise from the kitchen had ceased, and the whole building was deathly quiet, so quiet that we could hear the dog breathing just outside the door; from time to time he moaned. Far-off sounds of the woods drifted in through the window, beyond which we could see strips of starry sky between the bars.

"It really is like being in jail, isn't it?" she whispered after we had stared up through the little opening a while. "Almost like we're in another country in prison, waiting to be rescued or executed."

I turned up on an elbow and looked down at her. "How long has it been since we slept together on a single bed?"

"How long has it been since we slept together on *any* bed?" she returned.

"Good point. I kinda miss—well, you know, I just, I just occasionally think about the first year or so, when we had something, when I think that we really *had* something."

She squeezed my hand. "We don't have to talk about this. Let's just lie here watching what we can of the stars out there."

So we did, for what seemed like hours, her hand in mine, our breathing almost in unison. Outside our cell the night went on.

"You know," I leaned and whispered into her ear after a while, "I don't remember ever being in such complete silence."

"Me either. No cars passing. Nothing. It's unearthly."

"I was thinking the same thing."

"I noticed for the first time tonight," she said, snuggling up to me and throwing a leg across mine, "that you have eyes the color of a cat's, with little gold specks in them." She slid astride me and sat up, flinging her hair wildly about her head and giggling.

"Shhh, not so loud. Duke'll hear you. What are you doing?" I could not tell for certain in the subdued light of the room, but she appeared to be removing her blouse.

"Screw Duke." She threw the blouse into the crates, slipped her bra off, and stood up and removed her jeans. Her panties glowed like a quarter moon until she slid them down.

"Jesus, Annie, what are you doing?" Astraddle me, she had dropped to her knees and loosened my belt. She was sliding my pants off, shorts with them.

Then we were naked, our mouths hot on each other, our hands finding what our eyes could not in the dark. She remained on top of me, sliding and writhing, moaning as loudly as she dared, until we were united as we had not been in years, until we were a single thrusting animal rising in its pleasure toward a release that lay beyond the fear and darkness of that room.

Later, damp with perspiration and locked in each other's arms, we slept heavily until just at dawn we heard the old woman knock at the door.

After a breakfast of fried bologna, eggs, and boiled potatoes, a meal during which our eyes met only once, a brief, embarrassing glance of confusion, my wife and I rose from the table and asked permission to leave. With a mere nod of the head, the old woman consented without hesitation and ushered us to the door. She mentioned as she closed the screen door behind us that down the road half a mile or so there was a home where we could probably make a phone call. I thanked her and turned to catch up with my wife, who had already crossed the ravine and begun striding out, her shoes making little slapping sounds on the pavement.

"We can drive the car, you know, not fast, but we can drive it," I panted when I had caught up.

"No," she said, "I'd rather walk. The air feels good. I nearly suffocated in that damned storeroom."

We walked in silence for a while, until I finally summoned the nerve to say, "About last night . . ."

"Yes, she was crazy as hell—you know that? I really thought we would not get out of there alive."

"Annie, I mean—"

She stopped walking and grabbed my arm and turned me to face her. "Look, I was so insanely scared last night that I'm not certain I even remember what happened in that room. I don't want to think about that place, that room, and what happened in there. I don't know what got into us last night, so let's please keep walking and get the hell out of this Godforsaken country as soon as we can." She looked back toward the old building. "Or at least out of range of that damned pistol."

We walked on in silence and in the next bend saw at a distance the house the old woman had mentioned. I phoned from there and we sat and talked and had coffee with the young couple who rented the place while we waited for the auto club truck. We told them that we had spent the night with the old lady up the road, but when the wife said, smiling, "She seems like a nice woman, so very private," Annie and I exchanged glances and mentioned her no more. An hour and a half later the truck arrived and I rode with the driver to get the car.

As he put on a new tire I sat in the truck and watched the front of the house. Except for one brief movement of a curtain there was no sign of life in the building, but I knew that somewhere behind that wall of concrete blocks the old woman stood, the .44 hanging at one side, Duke hackled and growling at the other. I was relieved when finally I heard my trunk slam and the truck driver returned to the cab and announced that the car was ready to go.

I settled with him and picked up Annie and we headed off toward Houston through the corridor of woods that the young couple assured us we would soon break out of. The morning was deliciously cool, the recent heavy rains having been triggered by an early front, so we didn't use the air conditioner. The wind from her open window played in Annie's hair, making her look wonderfully young and desirable. I glanced over at her twice, but each time she turned to the wall of trees.

In a few miles the woods began to thin and stores appeared, houses and towers, apparitions in the morning sun, so ordinary to us a day ago and now as refreshing as the air from the windows, as the shocking blue of the sky, as my sudden memory of the night before. I looked at her again and slid my hand over to touch hers on the seat. Our fingers met and twined and she smiled as she turned to face me.

"I left my panties in those boxes somewhere," she said. "I couldn't find them."

"You left your panties? You're not wearing underwear?"

"Couldn't find them in all those crates and boxes."

"You wanna go back and get them?"

And then we laughed, laughed until tears streaked our faces, and the tension and terror of the night before faded as the morning air washed across us.

Still giggling, she clenched my hand and said, "We'll talk about last night. Later we'll talk about it."

STORM

F R O M about ten o'clock on, a cell blossomed steadily in the south, beyond the hill, building on itself until it stood one thin column of cloud, with the slightest orange mushrooming at the tip. The two of them, a man and woman well into middle age, leaned on hoes in their small, dusty garden, now so chastised by long days of sun and dry winds that there seemed little need in bothering to care for what few things remained alive. The beans were thin and pale, the squash wilted, tomatoes stunted. Little swirls of dust rose as they went back to their hoeing, reaching out and dragging bright blades, burnished by daily use and sharpened to half their original length, just beneath the soil crust. Sprigs of grass fell over and wilted almost immediately in the blasting sun.

"How can you tell it's a thunderstorm so soon," she asked after he had commented on it the third time, "and not some ordinary cloud?" She had stopped again and stood, propped on the hoe, watching the southern sky.

He turned from his hoeing beside her to say, "Because of its shape, behavior, the way it is updrafting."

She leaned and took a swipe at a patch of green. "It looks like some kind of flower, about to break out in color."

"That's the cumulus stage we're watching," he continued, "just sits there updrafting through the chimney, drawing moisture, developing the cell."

"Is it raining under it?" Sweat was beginning to seep into her eyes at the corners.

"No, just the opposite right now—sucking up moisture, like a kitchen sponge."

She reached her sleeve across and wiped the sweat away. "I wish someone would squeeze it out here, where it or one of its brothers has been sucking up our moisture for weeks on end, not returning a drop to us."

He hoed on in silence for a while, then answered, "Well, someone will get rain later, somewhere, when the cell's matured on up in the day, probably over around Livingston, where they don't need it."

After lunch they climbed to the top of the hill that rose from the edge of their back yard and sat under an oak to watch the storm. Behind them their square little house sat boldly in white at the edge of the browning pastures that stretched out from the foot of the hill and ended at the dark green border of the creek, which always managed a trickle in the harshest of droughts. A handful of lean cattle worked their heads in and out of the brush at the creek edge, and a spiral of buzzards turned lazily above them, drifting along with the wind.

A stranger passing where they sat would have remarked that what he looked down on had to be one of the sorriest East Texas farms he had ever seen: small, drought-parched, poorly fenced, outbuildings faded and flimsy, the house so small that passage from the front to back door could be made in five good bounds. And he would have wondered what could keep two people out here, in obvious poverty, to battle with the inimical forces of nature when there must be better lives for them somewhere else. And certainly there were better farms to be had.

But they would not have cared what he said. They were there by choice, gave up affluent lives in the city, walked away from a world of options, preferring a life of stark simplicity. They were products of the sixties, free spirits, he with a braided tail of hair yet, though it was streaked with gray, and she a lean, weathered woman whose arms and legs were knotted with hard muscles, her face ravaged by sun and wind. And the farm, pitiful as it might be, was theirs, paid for, and it satisfied them. That was what mattered. They were who and where they wanted to be, and though they had long since—and with pleasure—eschewed the foggy world of drugs and eastern philosophies and open social protest, they never regretted their retreat to the country, except when nature, in one of her malevolent streaks, countered every move they made.

The storm was thickening now and beginning to boil with what she supposed looked like anger, if a storm could be angry or nature could be unkind.

"There seems sometimes to be an unfairness about all this," he said quietly, "the way the sky takes away our water day after day and carries it off to someone else, who we do not know and who may not even need it."

"There's a balance in things, I guess." She watched while the top of the storm flattened out like hair whipping out from a girl's head. She could feel a freshening in the air from the direction of the storm, a stirring of her long brown hair. There were times like this, when she sat in silence and watched the changing face of the sky, that she imagined what their children would have been like, had they managed to have them: the boys tall and lean like their father, with feathery brown eyes and skewed smile, the girls like her, willowy and pretty in a plain way, hair fine as smoke. But she did not allow herself to wander long in the sky, stopping always short of the precipitous plunge into aching emptiness.

He pointed: "That's the anvil forming on top. The storm's fatter and darker now, and you can tell which way it's moving by the anvil."

"Which way do you think it's moving?" she asked, not in challenge.

"Away from us, off to the west, but I would have known that anyway, without the anvil."

"You're being cynical again. It may come back." He had in recent years voiced a darker side than she had ever known him to have; he smiled less. She worried about it sometimes. Once in one of his foul moods, brought on as usual by extended dry weather, he declared that he was ready to give it all up and move back to the city. "I feel so incredibly earthbound," he had said, driving his boot heel down onto the dry, hard soil. "Dark, earth-colored, like a corpse turning back into clay." But she coaxed him out of his despair, loving and reassuring him as she always had. Still, the moods came so sudden on him now, and so often.

"Let's get some more rows done." He picked up his hoe and started back down the hill, turning to look once more at the widening storm. "Somebody is really getting a shower." He pointed to the dark streaks under the belly of the storm. "A solid curtain of rain."

They hoed on in the midafternoon heat until he shaded his eyes toward the sun and announced that it was time for other chores.

"Before we get on with other things, can we rest?" she asked him as they walked to the barn. It was not that she was really tired. The work would always be there, whenever they turned to it, the cycle of chores as endless as the seasons, so she felt no urgency, no compelling haste. That was the attitude they had agreed on in the beginning, and she had kept the agreement.

"Sure," he told her, "why don't we watch other folks get rain?"

She pointed up to the loft. "Let's go up there." They lay then across the bales of hay and looked out to the south, where the storm was grumbling and tossing about. Years earlier what happened next would have been as predictable as sunrise, but now they merely lay side by side, touching each other but without passion, like two shoes set in a closet.

"It's already dispersing," he pointed out, "see how the black is fading out of it?"

"It seems closer."

"Seems but isn't," he said. "Just wider and taller."

"It *sounds* closer," she persisted. The curtain of rain seemed to be drawing toward them, the trees were whipping and thrashing along the creek, the sun was fading. "I believe that it is going to rain on us."

For an answer he slid off the hay and backed down the ladder. "Well, I don't," he told her as he started off down toward the pasture bottom. "You stay up there where you can be dry, if you believe that it's going to rain. I've got to go check the fence down there where the bull broke through last week."

She watched him cross the pasture, a weak shadow rippling along beside him and slightly behind like some pursuing ghost, and disappear into the brush that bordered the creek just as the sun darkened and a solid curtain of rain slid across the hill. He burst out of the green wall when the rain reached him, his hands out and spread to the flashing, rumbling sky, as if he would gather in the whole storm. The barn roof drummed with heavy drops, then roared. The last she saw of her husband before the storm swallowed him, he was running in wide circles, his face aglow, hair trailing straight out behind, arms spread like some enchanted boy trying hard to fly.

THE
DEPUTY

WHEN the call came that morning, the first time the phone had rung since his arrival at the office, Sheriff Earl White was staring across his desk at his deputy's young face, marveling at how pale it was for someone just out of high school and summer well underway in East Texas. He ought to be bronzed up like some kind of god instead of looking like something that had been living out of the sun all its life. He just didn't look quite right.

And there was that little sideways jut of jaw that threw his narrow chin out at an angle, giving him the appearance of a perpetual pout, though White had known the boy to be nothing but pleasant and agreeable, even silly, a good part of the time. Just a farm boy, little more, with a smattering of education from a nearby junior college and an aversion to haying and plowing, which was more or less what White had been himself when, thirty years before, he began as a deputy two counties over. The boy needed meat on him, a good woman, and a few years dealing with the ignorance and passions of the country poor—he might or might not be around long enough to grow into what could at best be described as a mediocre job in a mediocre town in a mediocre county in what White was beginning to feel was a mediocre state, land of the Texas Rangers or not.

The phone startled him. It didn't ring often enough for him to regard it likely that it would ever ring again when he'd hung up; and when it did ring, the possibility that the call was of any importance was negligible. Somebody's cow had got through barbed wire and was standing in the road and causing a traffic hazard—wouldn't he come and help put it up, if he wasn't too busy?

And he, of course, never was, since in a town with eight traffic lights and a county with just a few thousand people, there wasn't that much to be busy doing. As a matter of fact, he didn't really guess he was needed at all—two full-time policemen and four reserve officers could manage the town, and the constables, such as they were, seemed to keep the peace well enough in the county. Things had always had a way of settling themselves out there. Still, he was there, along with his new deputy, and when the phone rang it was his to answer.

When he hung up, he looked over at the deputy, who was reading a *National Inquirer,* and said, "Simms, I reckon you could do with a little sun, so I want you to make a run out in the country for me."

The deputy thrust his jaw to the side and lowered his newspaper. "Sure. What's up?"

White swung his legs up onto his desk and leaned back in his chair, grinning. "Seems like Peter Pumphrey plucked his pecker out'n his pocket—in front of somebody's wife."

The younger man laid his paper down and folded it neatly. "Say what?"

"Old Will Pumphrey's boy exposed himself in front of Dr. Cole's wife while her and a friend was out picking berries and—"

"In the country?"

White nodded his head. "Of course in the country. Out on Route Five, not far from where the Pumphreys live. Cole and them's got a little place out there. Nothing much on it, just an old house and some scattered fruit trees and berry bushes and what have you. Pretty much growed over. Her and a friend was

picking some berries when young Pumphrey stood up from behind some bushes and whipped it out in front of them."

"Was he peeing, or what?" The deputy was grinning too now.

"Seems like he was working on it while he was studying them.
They was scared he was going to try to rape'm or something and
hauled it out of there. Cole's mad as hell and wants to press
charges."

"Sheriff," Simms said, rising to get his hat, "if I had known I
was getting into this life-and-death kind of police work I never
would have signed on." He slipped his pistol belt off the back of
his chair and held it up. "I guess I'll take my gun, given the seri-
ousness of this case."

"Damned right you'll take it, boy, and the shotgun. I don't
want you making any kind of call without having your weapons
with you. And—set down a second." He lowered his feet to the
floor and looked intently at the deputy.

"Look, Simms, if I didn't have to spend some time over at the
courthouse this morning, I'd go out there and do this myself."

"You don't think I can—"

"Don't go anticipating me, son. I know you can handle this;
otherwise I'd go myself, courthouse stuff or not. But Pumphrey,
the old man, is bad news. Real bad. He's killed a couple of people in his life. Been in all kinds of trouble over the years, though
he ain't never give me a whole lot, mainly because I inherited
him after he was too old to cause much. When he was younger,
though, he was damn mean. He's just old and probably a little
crazy now, and dumb, which don't combine well with meanness
for the man that's got to deal with him. And them kids are
mean too. Even the women—wife and older girls and aunts,
whatever and whoever the hell they are. Cliff, they ain't to be
messed with." White pressed his fists on the desk and leaned
forward.

"You drive up to the edge of the yard and tell the old man—
he'll probably be setting on the porch—that you want to speak
to Pete, and you talk the boy into coming back with you. Tell
him he's got to come in and see me is all, right now. I figger I

can talk Cole out of filing charges, if the boy will come in and apologize."

"You don't want me to arrest him?" Simms, leaning back in his chair, was squinting at some specks of rust on the shotgun.

"You are to drive up into the edge of the yard and tell the old man that you want to speak to Pete, and then you talk the boy into getting into the car and coming back with you. That's all. If he won't come, you get on back here and I'll go out and see what I can do."

"Yessir. I'm on my way." He plopped his hat on and smiled and headed out.

"Cliff." White motioned him back. He reached and placed one of his hands on the deputy's shoulder. "Cliff, you do this just like I told you. You hear?"

"Got you, Sheriff." He threw a cocky little salute with two fingers and spun sharply on the ball of his left foot and got into the car. He leaned and rolled the passenger window down. "I'll be real sure Peter puts his pecker up before I get back to town with him." He laughed and rolled up the window and started his engine.

White watched the deputy turn the patrol car around and ease out into the street. He stared after him until the car disappeared around a corner, then went back into the office and sat down and studied the wall across from his desk. Mean. That's what the old man was, mean. The whole family, from the leathery patriarch down to the youngest child, a girl of five or so that he had sired when he was nearly seventy. A pit of vipers, nest of hornets, whatever you could think of that was vicious and stubborn and doggedly territorial and intolerant of anyone that wasn't one of them—that's what the Pumphreys were.

And Jesus, maybe he shouldn't have sent the boy out there. But he had to start somewhere, and so far he hadn't done anything but write a couple of traffic tickets and serve some papers. Might as well throw him into the pen with the baddest dog and see how he came out.

Still, Simms was so young and naive and had never faced anything like old Pumphrey, and, Goddamn it, White had come to feel like the boy was his own, his own son. Which you weren't supposed to do. You hired somebody as a deputy to do the work you didn't want to do yourself—the dirty and tedious and unsavory stuff—and you didn't care one way or the other whether he liked it or not. You could pick up a deputy in five minutes any damned where in the county and teach him in another five all he needed to know to do a halfway decent job. And you damned sure weren't supposed to worry about him when he went off to bring in a little redneck that didn't have any better sense than to try to whip off in front of a doctor's wife.

And maybe if the boy were going anywhere other than to the Pumphrey place he wouldn't worry. He stared out across the street and remembered he was supposed to be at the courthouse soon, so he closed the door to the office and locked it and started toward the old stained brick building that rose out of the trees like a medieval fortress, within which, packed in file cabinets heavy with the tedious dust of time, the county records were kept. To him that courthouse was the only permanent symbol of authority and order in the county, everything else merely temporary and expendable, and without it and its records and agents life for ordinary people would be impossible. He supposed that his greatest satisfaction in life was being part of the power and stability it represented. When he wasn't doing something official over there, he was sitting around joking with judges and lawyers and the old men who draped themselves along the benches that ran around the perimeter of the block. That was part of being a small-town sheriff. That was the way you *kept* being a small-town sheriff.

He stood watching the street for a few minutes, nodding at the scattered traffic, then stepped off the curb. There was no use thinking about sending Simms out there now. He was gone. And he would do what he was told. So damned young and inexperienced, so unaware, yet good at taking orders, and that was what mattered most. Hell, you could take boys just out of high school and whip them into effective soldiers in six weeks if they could just take orders. Men did the thinking for boys—they were just supposed to do what they were told. Even if it meant going out and meeting for the first time one of the meanest men you could imagine.

It was easy enough to remember his first trip out to the Pumphrey place. The old man, in his sixties then, had had a falling-out with the utility company over some tree trimming along the road and ordered the crew of trimmers to leave, using a shotgun to get his point across. They radioed their supervisor, who called White, and, whether he liked it or not, he had to go out there. At the time the county could not afford to provide him with a full-time deputy.

He had pulled up into the driveway and shut off his engine, letting Pumphrey come to him, if he would—he felt terribly uneasy stepping out onto the land of these people, though he knew almost every one of them by name and face. There was no one on the porch, but he knew the old man was probably peeping from a window. The only thing White could do was get out of the car and approach the house or sit there and wait. So he waited.

How long he sat there, he could not have told anyone, but he counted half a dozen buzzards spiraling at different places in the sky at different times and watched the sun drag a windshield pock a full inch across the dash before anything moved at the house. A curtain cracked, he was sure, and he had turned to study that window when the screen door squawked open and Pumphrey stepped out, barefooted, and stood looking at him. White motioned him to the car and the old man swung down off the porch and in three strides stood, one arm on the roof of the car above the door, towering over him.

Before a single word could be said, before White had even ducked his head down enough to look into Pumphrey's eyes, the curtain cracked again and a gun barrel slid out on the ledge, its muzzle slowly dropping until it pointed at White's face. It happened so fast, so slowly, that what followed was a series of still frames in his memory: his hand slamming onto his revolver, fumbling at the holster snap, his body falling back on the seat to make a smaller target and allow him to raise the pistol, between the curtains a great expanse of white face into which a black gun barrel seemed to have been driven like a stake, and the old man's voice booming down on him: "Don't shoot him, don't shoot him, it won't shoot, it's broke, don't shoot."

And then, his body flattened against the passenger-side door, he was staring up the barrel of his cocked revolver, past the old man's twisted mouth and white eyes, his front sight darting and weaving like a needle on the flat, wide face between the curtains.

"It's just the boy, the *boy*. It won't shoot, the gun won't shoot!" Pumphrey was yelling, his neck stretched out like a thick, skin-covered rope, his stubbled red face contorted around his open mouth. He had moved his body between the gun at the window and the gun in the car and crouched low with White's revolver aimed dead at his flaring gray left eye.

"Tell him to put it down, throw the gun out the window," White said, his voice a strange mixture of authority and supplication. The old man turned, sweeping his arm as if he would brush away the house itself, and yelled for the women to get the boy out of the window and take the gun away from him and throw it out. The face disappeared as if by magic, the curtains fell to, and then an enormous black-brown pistol flew from the window and landed halfway between White's car and the house. It sounded to him like an anvil hitting the ground.

"He don't mean nothing by it, Sheriff, it's just a toy to him, been playing with it since he was a little feller." He held out a quivering hand and lowered it until it came to a point halfway up his thigh. "Just knee high when I give it to him to play with—it wasn't no good—and he ain't turned loose of it since."

"Still," White answered, his eyes on the pistol in the dust.

"It's broke inside and rusted and the cylinder won't even turn. He'd have to chunk it and hit you with it to hurt you."

"Still, Pumphrey, it is a gun and folks can't tell at a distance what will shoot and what won't. That barrel looks just as big on a broke gun as on a good one." He stared up at the old man, whose hard gray eyes had turned soft and filmy, almost feminine. "Pumphrey, I could have blowed him out of that window. I come that close." He held his thumb and forefinger half an inch apart, but the gap pulsed with the pounding of his heart, still stuck in the back of his throat somewhere.

Pumphrey shook his head. "I know it, damn it, don't I know it?" He turned toward the porch and took a few steps before turning back around to face the sheriff. "And you and me both know what I would have had to do if you *had* of killed him, don't we? I'll be in in the morning to talk to you about what you come out here about. You won't have to come back out here."

And he was good as his word. He came to White's office the next morning with a hulking teenage boy, flaccid as a toad, who shuffled across the floor to the sheriff's desk, his head down and tears dripping onto his shirt front.

"This is Willy, Sheriff," the old man said, pushing the boy forward until his soiled pants touched the front of the desk. "It was him had the gun. He's come to apologize for pointing it at you." He nudged the boy, who, chin still down on his shirt front, mumbled something that White took to be an apology. Pumphrey spun him around at that and shoved him toward the door, still partly open, where a lean female arm reached through and grasped him and pulled him out of the office.

"He ain't quite right, Sheriff. He ain't ever been quite right. He's just a baby in the head and probably won't ever be nothing more. He never meant nothing with that damned Colt. It's an old cap-and-ball that I've let him play with since he was just a tyke. He couldn't load it even if it *would* shoot, which it won't. We take'n it away from him time and time again, but he sets up such a beller that the women always give in and give it back." He scratched his neck and looked down at his hands. "You just do the best you can, y'know."

And that was as far as it went. For a few minutes White felt genuinely sorry for the old man, until they got off into a discussion about the tree-trimming matter, which degenerated into a fiery exchange that left him hating Pumphrey and his whole tribe. He couldn't even remember exactly how the issue was settled, except that old Pumphrey obviously wasn't satisfied and left with the declaration that next time he'd blow the trimmers out of the trees like possums.

A blaring truck horn down the block brought him back, but the image of the face in the window was still on his mind as he crossed the street toward the courthouse. Trouble was, for some strange reason he kept seeing between the curtains not the moon-faced idiot boy but the pale, narrow face of his deputy.

He had just taken a step onto the sidewalk when he stopped and stared at the sky, then retraced his steps to the office, where, even before he opened the door, he could hear a frantic voice on the radio.

Simms shut off the engine and motioned for the old man on the porch, who still had not moved except to turn his head in the general direction of the patrol car when it pulled into the yard. They sat looking at each other a few minutes, then Pumphrey dropped his feet from the railing where they had been propped and stood, stretched, and spat across a row of sorry-looking flowers that had been planted just out from the porch. The old man sat back down and laced his hands behind his head. "What you want?" he yelled. He was looking out across the road.

Simms lowered his window and leaned his head out into the hot air. "Sir?"

"I said, what do you want?"

"Mr. Pumphrey—you are Mr. Pumphrey, aren't you?" He took off his sunshades and laid them on the dash. "Sure hot, ain't it?"

"I am, and it is. It's summer, ain't it? Now, what do you want?" He still seemed totally uninterested, his gaze moving across the road, then to Simms, then to his bare feet, which he had raised again to the rail.

"Sheriff White sent me out here to ask your son, Pete, to come in and talk with him about something that happened over at Dr. Cole's place." Simms had opened his door and put one foot onto the ground. "There's—"

"Ain't nothing happened over at the Cole place that Pete said nothing to me about. You got the wrong boy, I guess."

"Well, no sir, I think I've got it right. Pete is the one I need to talk to." He had just dropped his other foot to the ground and reached for his hat when he saw a motion, a shadow, something

36

at the corner of the house to his left. Then he knew it was a man or large boy, massive and slow like some heavy farm animal lumbering along, and dangling from his right hand was a pistol.

Simms swung his feet back into the car and slammed the door in one motion, staring, unbelieving, as the boy stumbled toward the car, slowly lifting the pistol until it was aimed directly at the window that framed the deputy's face. Instinctively Simms reached for his service revolver, fumbled with it for what seemed like a full minute, all the while staring into the barrel of the pistol, then yanked the shotgun from its spring clip on the dash, pumping as he raised it, and thrust it through the open door. He was vaguely aware that the old man had slung his chair across the porch and leaped toward the car.

He knew that he fired twice before cranking the car and putting it in gear and spinning around in the yard and out onto the road, but how many more times he shot he did not know until he saw jiggling along the windshield on the dash three bright red shells. The smell of burned gunpowder filled the car. He could hear nothing over the roaring in his ears.

Only when he was out of sight of the house and had stabilized the fishtailing car did he have the presence of mind to radio for help. He shouted first for an ambulance, though he knew from the way the boy blew back from the car and crumpled like a headshot cow that the shotgun had struck him full force, maybe more than once. The roar in his ears was so loud that the voice answering him came muffled as if from some great distance. Then he called for White.

"Sheriff, Sheriff, come in. Can you hear me? You got to get out here."

When he had reached the highway White had still not answered, so he swung the car around and parked on the dirt road, aimed back toward the Pumphrey place, to wait for the ambulance, which had to come from Lufkin, at least a fifteen-minute drive. He radioed White again and again, each time fighting to keep his voice under control.

Finally the radio came back, "I got you loud and clear, boy. Slow down now and tell me what's happened out there."

"Earl, I shot him, the Pumphrey boy. I—Earl, you got to get out here."

"You shot *Pete* or the dumb one?" He leaned and yanked his pistol belt off the coatrack. "Never mind, Cliff. You just hang on. I'm on my way."

Just as he reached the intersection of the caliche road that led off into the low hills in which the Pumphreys lived White saw the flashing lights of the ambulance coming from the other direction. Simms's patrol car was parked on the edge of the dirt road, pointed away from the highway. He slowed just enough to make a safe turn and slid in behind the deputy, who stood with one foot on the ground, the other on the floorboard of the car, gesturing toward two vehicles, a reddish truck and green car, that had just topped the hill in front of him. They bore down like oversized toys flung by some enraged child from behind the curtain of woods that closed beyond the hill.

As the ambulance swung in behind the patrol cars and lurched to a stop in a boil of dust, the two vehicles reached the intersection, the driver of the truck staring straight ahead, his eyes black and fierce beneath a brown hat brim. Someone leaned against the opposite door, supporting a head that rolled across the back glass of the cab, a great pale head topped with a shock of dark hair. And then they were past and the car, full of children and women, squealed onto the highway and followed the truck on out of sight.

Simms was slouched back onto the front seat of the car when White and the ambulance driver and his assistant panted up.

The sheriff grabbed the deputy's arm. "Was that them?"

Simms looked at him, his mind as blank as the white sky that seemed to press down on the trees behind the hill. "That was them."

"Did you see the one you shot?"

"Yessir. They had him in the cab. Between them. Between the old man and the boy."

"Which one—"

"What are we supposed to do?" the ambulance driver broke in. Do you want—"

"Just wait a damn minute and we'll let you know," White answered quietly, tightening his grip on Simms's arm. "Now tell me, boy, which one did you shoot?" His eyes were locked on the three shells that had vibrated into a tight little cluster on the passenger's side of the dash.

"I don't *know* who I shot. It was the one in the middle, the big one, the big fat one."

"Oh, sweet Jesus." White released his arm and turned to the ambulance driver. "They take'n him on to the hospital, I reckon, so there ain't nothing y'all can do out here. You might as well get on back to Lufkin and be sure that that rattle-ass truck and car makes it in with him. We going on out to the house and try to get straight on what happened. See what you can find out from the hospital about his condition and give me a call back soon as you can. And keep quiet about this."

The driver nodded and motioned his assistant back to the ambulance. They spun out into the highway, lights and siren going, and headed back to town.

The two of them sat in White's car at the edge of the yard where Simms had been parked. There was no sign of life in the house. The front door stood open.

"This is about where you were?" White asked.

"About here. Maybe a few feet further up. But about here." Simms pointed to the front porch. "The old man was there on the porch."

"And where was *he?*"

Simms pointed straight out the window on White's side. "He come from around that corner right there, like some kind of big animal or something, like a shadow or a ghost—I just couldn't tell. He had a gun."

White looked where he pointed, his eyes coming to rest on a raw gash up about four feet where some of the buckshot from the deputy's gun had struck the corner of the paintless house, weathered an almost even gray by decades of rain and sun and wind. Halfway between the corner and the car a dark spot as big as a washtub had stained the hard-packed dirt. White pointed with his foot. "That where he landed?"

Simms nodded but said nothing.

"How many times did you shoot him?"

"I don't know. More than once."

"There was three shells on your dash. Them come from your gun?" White was still staring at the dark spot in the dirt.

"Yessir. So I guess I shot him three times."

"I guess so," the sheriff said, getting out and walking over to the corner of the house. He turned and looked back at Simms, who had remained in the car.

"It was some kind of big black pistol he had. It looked big as a hog's leg."

White turned toward the woods and watched the sky press down until he could feel his breath thinning. He had never been past the edge of the yard before, but he knew how it would look behind the house: the broken-back barn and leaning cribs and outbuildings, sagging fences, two bowed clotheslines from which hung a few pieces of stained and faded wash that the women must have strung out that morning. Two aged milk cows grazed in the near pasture, pinching off the stubby, sparse grass, while off in the distance, beyond the barn and pens, a stolid mule stared toward the strange man in khaki who stood at the corner of the house. A rusting tractor missing a rear tire sat propped up on concrete blocks near the barn. Everything looked so incredibly worn-out and old, as if some ancient violation of nature had yielded this pitiful lifetime bounty, the myriad bits and pieces of decay that began at the horizon and played out only when the old man's property ended at the road. He started toward the outbuildings, thought better of it, then returned to the front yard. Simms was still sitting where he had left him.

When he finally walked back to the car, he said quietly as he got in, "Son, you shot Willy, the idiot, and what he was waving at you was that damn Colt Dragoon that he's been playing with since he was in diapers. And," he added as he turned the car around, "a real hog's leg would have been just as serious a threat as that pistol." He sighed. "But you couldn't have known that."

The ambulance driver didn't radio any news, so White drove to the office and, while the deputy filled out his report in a back room, called the hospital to check on the condition of the boy. He had little doubt what the news would be.

Just as the sheriff hung up, Simms stepped into the room. All the color was gone from his face, had been gone all afternoon. White remembered that when he drove up behind the deputy's car out there he was struck by the total lack of color in the younger man's face. Like he'd seen a ghost.

"Is he—is he dead?"

White whirled and faced him. "Is he *dead?* My God, son, you fired three rounds of double-ought buckshot into that boy, and you have to ask whether he's dead? There ain't an animal on this earth that could take that kind of punishment and still be alive."

"Then he is dead." Simms walked to the window and looked out.

White stared past him at the steadily broadening sun that squatted, orange and angry, on the edge of the late-afternoon sky. The deputy's outline darkened the window. "All we can do now is wait," he said softly. "Might as well sit down."

The sun, then, began its slow settle to the west while the two men waited, each with his own thoughts, on one side of the desk the heavy, aging one, on the other the slender youth, face ashen, his lean jaw trapped between two hands that would have trembled visibly had he not held them tightly vised. Before either of them spoke again, the sun stretched out the shadow of an engraved .45 cartridge stood up on end on White's desk until the round tip of the bullet had elongated and slid halfway across the desk, aiming, it seemed to White, right at the boy's chest. A memento from the American Legion, the cartridge had sat on his desk for years, doing that same thing every day that the sun came through the window; he had never noticed the way its shadow stretched out and swung like some dark pointing finger.

"When he comes," the sheriff said finally, so low that Simms had to lean to hear him, "you are to go into the back room and stay there. I'll say whatever has to be said. I'll handle it."

"You think he'll come, then."

"He'll come. Oh, yeah. I don't know when or how, or who or what he'll bring with him or how it'll turn out. But he'll come." He shifted his weight in the chair.

"I just don't understand all this, Earl. I did the only thing that I could do under the circumstances. He come at me with a gun that looked real enough, and I never had time to make a judgment on whether it would shoot or not. It looked—"

"Just hush, Cliff. You ain't got to defend yourself to me. I know—I been there." But he did not tell the deputy about the face in the window, the broad, bovine face that he had almost blown away a decade before. He had never told anyone. No point in it. Nor did he tell him what might happen when the old man came.

"You expecting real trouble from him, ain't you?" Simms asked.

White reached out and scooped up the cartridge, whose shadow had all but crossed the desk. "He's old, Cliff, and crazy, and ain't got anything to live for but that nest of women and kids, and he could be trouble, yeah. He's reached the point where don't nothing much matter to him. And, Jesus, half the people outside the lights of this town would kill you over a glass of iced tea. It's just how they are. You just go on hoping nothing like this ever happens." He rubbed his hand over his face. "But sometimes it does."

After that they lapsed into silence again. To think about the ways of the people, the ways of the world that was theirs—by choice, by necessity, but theirs, as certain as breath itself. And those who escaped it, to travel deep into the bowels of the city or off into the sparse west or into other states and countries, never really escaped it, the violence and passions of the people. It came simply in another form, as one storm, shrieking with lightning and wind, is different from another only in the direction it comes from and in its magnitude, ravaging unabated until it has worn itself out with the fury built up in it. You can run from it or hide from it, but it will run its course. Which is all right, White was thinking, only because there's nothing to do about it anyway. If only you could keep it from the children.

"Oh, Jesus, Earl—it's the old man, it's Pumphrey. His truck just pulled up." Simms had just been standing at the window watching the evening sky, his hands to his sides, limp, like someone resigned to take whatever blows are coming. He turned to White. "What do I do?"

White stood and squinted out the window. "You don't do anything at all except go into the back room like I told you. And set down and keep quiet."

In what now was early evening, Pumphrey's truck was parked out front. News of the shooting had not spread to town apparently, so there was no traffic about, no one standing on sidewalk corners to watch the showdown—even the courthouse had been closed down for the day and darkened. The old man got out and stood beside his truck a minute, then leaned back in and pulled out a heavy black pistol. Someone still sat in the truck on the passenger's side.

White turned from the window and resumed his seat, staring straight ahead at the door behind which his deputy sat, young, uncertain, and terrified. He glanced from his pistol belt hanging on the rack to the two shotguns locked in the cabinet with the rifles, but he made no move to arm himself. When the door opened, he strangely felt no surge of fear, only fatigue.

The old man's voice came slow, as if each word had to rise through layers of heavy emotion. "I got one boy over at a funeral home in Lufkin and one in the truck. You done took one away from me today and I've brought in the other. I ain't got any fight left in me, White. I'm too old to try to fight you, or your boy."

He stood before the sheriff with his hat in his right hand, gesturing weakly like someone trying to explain an old wrong that he knows cannot be justified with words. A large brown-black revolver dangled at his side from the other hand. His eyes were red with crying, glazed, and he looked straight through the sheriff, it seemed, right through the wall behind him and on off into some great distance of time and space.

Behind the old man a rawboned boy, probably in his midteens, leaned in the doorway, his head hung in shame or grief or simple surrender—White couldn't tell. His shirt, once probably a dark blue but faded to a bird-egg pale gray, had a plate-sized splotch of dark blood on it, and little tentacles of brighter blood radiated from the center, forming a design that looked absurdly like something a sister might have done for him as a favor with dye.

White glanced at the pistol, then nodded to the boy. "This Pete?" He had never seen the boy up close before, only skulking on the porch or off behind the house the few times he had had occasion to drive by the Pumphrey place. The old man nodded and gestured with his hat again. The boy cut his eyes up at his father, not in fear or anger but in what the sheriff could only read as perplexity.

"Mr. Pumphrey," White began, "ain't nobody sorrier about all this than me and the deputy. It didn't have to happen, *shouldn't* have, but it did and we got to live with what comes out of it. That boy back there—" He motioned to the door of the room in which Simms sat. "The boy didn't know about that old pistol. It looked real enough to him, and your boy—"

The old man held the gun out to White. "I take'n this gun away from him a dozen times, twice this year, and even throwed it in the cattle tank a few weeks ago, but he set up such a beller that the women went out and got it and washed it off and give it back to'm. He never liked no toy the way he liked this old Colt."

White nodded, turning to glance at the red western sky.

"I give it to him when he was—I don't know, maybe four or five, and he's loved it ever since. Slept with it even."

"I know, Mr. Pumphrey, I know about all that, but that boy back there just didn't know . . ."

"Sheriff, nothing on it works, it won't cock, and even if it had of worked, Willy couldn't of loaded a black-powder pistol and shot it. It's just a wore-out, broke Dragoon, just a heavy piece of iron shaped like a pistol. My great-granddaddy picked it up on the way back from Mississippi after the War. I don't think that anybody in the family ever shot it."

White held the pistol and shook his head. "I know, I know about the pistol. Remember? But my boy didn't. To him it was any other pistol in another man's hand, something that would blow a great big hole in him if he didn't get a shot off first."

"He shot him three times, White."

"He didn't even know how many times he shot. He was scared to death. I had to count the shells in the car before he knew."

The old man tried to speak again, but his voice failed, and he merely looked out the window toward the deep reddish-purple sky.

"Mr. Pumphrey, there's nothing can be done about your boy. This was clear-cut self-defense, and we both know it. There'll be a formal investigation and all, but I want this thing done and forgot, the best we can. You take Pete on back with you. And this." He handed him the old revolver. "You need to keep it as some sort of reminder." He wasn't sure what he meant by that, and Pumphrey looked uncertain when he accepted the gun. "I reckon we've all had enough trouble for one day. I'll talk to Dr. Cole about that other matter and get him to drop the charges. If you don't hear from me—and I don't expect you will—just figure it's been settled."

Pumphrey nodded. "I—" he began, then shrugged and glanced at the door behind which Simms was sitting. A scar, White noticed, ran deep and dark from the edge of his hairline above his right eye across to his left cheek and down past his ear, and he wondered what put it there, what old wound, in what outrage he had gotten it. Something was settling heavy in his chest now, like night itself, and he felt almost like reaching out and touching the old man, holding him, comforting him. Instead, he motioned toward the door. "Take your son, and go on home. Let's let this rest."

Pumphrey stood rigid and silent, like something cut from stone, one arm dangling at his side, hand cradling the old revolver, the other hand holding his hat, stretched out toward

White as if in supplication. When nothing else was said, he took a deep breath and left, easing the door to behind him.

The deputy did not hear all that was said. He sat in the quiet little room, flanked with file cabinets and shelves that held the testimony of a century of blood and grief, and listened to mur-murings beyond the door that he dared not open. He could hear no bitterness, no violence in their words, just the soft talk of old men, low and somnolent, trailing to nothing, like darkness set-tling on the land or the imperceptible yet certain gathering weight of time.

THE
RETURN

So it came to pass that in that year, the year he refused to celebrate his fiftieth birthday, he spurned the pleas of his friends and remonstrations of his wife of over twenty years and returned to the hills of Northwest Alabama and the old home place. One bright Saturday afternoon in late October the wheels of his car tracked through the first fallen leaves under the trees that lined the road before the house—and he was there.

Behind him, piled to the headliner, were suitcases and sacks of clothes, tools and odds and ends wedged wherever they would stay, and behind all that the trunk, so stuffed that he had had to use a length of wire to keep the lid below his field of vision to the rear. Beside him sat his wife, a sad little woman, thin and pretty yet, but worn hard into middle age, whose only words were, once the wheels had stopped, "Now what?"

They sat for a long while listening and looking at the front of the house. The engine cooled, popping and cracking, and now and then little gusts of wind topped the hill and swayed the car, its shadow slowly lengthening toward the edge of the porch. Neither spoke for a very long time.

Behind them, across the gravel road from the house, a small pasture lay in a strip between the woods and road; it was separated from a larger pasture by a barn and other outbuildings and a series of pens. He could see from his rearview mirror that all was overgrown—bushes and trees higher than a man's head dotted the pastures and pens. Behind the house, neglected fields, clumped with brush and trees, sloped off to walls of bright-green pines in three directions.

The house itself, ringed by oaks and hickories, sat on a knoll of bedrock sheeted by a veneer of red clay so barren and worn and hardened by generations of children that it was more like stone than dirt—grass roots had not penetrated it in decades, and the enriching leaves that fell each year merely blew off the ridge to accumulate against whatever stretches of hog wire and chicken wire remained from old garden plots down the hill. Paintless now, roof browned with rust, the old two-story house towered against the sky. It appeared to lean vaguely to the right like an aging man uncertain of his footing. No unbroken windows remained on the front or ends, stones from the road having long since shattered or pocked them, and the front door lay on the hall floor. As they got out of the car he could see through the long corridor to the rear that the back door was off its hinges as well and that piles of refuse cluttered the hallway.

"How long has it been since anybody lived here?" She was standing away from the porch like someone trying to edge upwind of something foul in the air. He was sitting on the top step.

"The last I heard, a family of Negroes was here, two or three years ago. Before them another family of Negroes. Before that—I don't know, some white trash trying to make a go of it as farmers." He pressed down on the end of one of the porch boards and found it surprisingly solid; veins of rich red-orange shone in the wood.

She still stood off from him, glancing at the weather-scarred front of the house. "How long since your folks were here?"

He pulled his knees up to his chest like a boy and stared off at the sagging ridge of the barn. "Over twenty years. They, my grandparents, died within a year of each other and the family sold the place to a timber firm, who cut the woods over and then leased the homesite and fields, the fifty acres we just bought, to whoever wanted to give it a go. They've replanted the cut areas. You can see the young pines across the road there and over in those hills." He pointed off to the bright green semicircle of new forest that arched from the horizon where the road disappeared in both directions. "They'll be able to cut them in another fifteen years or so."

She moved beside him and sat down on the step below the one he was on. "I still can't understand why we had to buy it, why you couldn't just come back and visit and let it go at that." She looked up at him.

"Mary Ann, it wouldn't be the same. It just wouldn't." He stared past her at the outbuildings across the road. "I wanted to return, to come back to where I came from. It's just—well, I've reached that point of my life when . . ." He sighed and held his hands out in appeal. "I can't explain any better than I already have."

"You really don't have to talk about it, Jim. You've said it all before, and now we've done it. It's kind of like finally jumping off a cliff that you've been afraid you'd jump off of for years. Once you've taken that last step, you can't undo it. You just hope you don't land too hard. The place is ours and we're here and even if I don't understand, I'll try to keep my mouth shut and go along."

"I mean, my great-grandparents built this house right after the Civil War—God only knows how they did it—and after they died, my grandparents took the farm over. My father lived here and even, for a while, my mother, and I spent every vacation of my childhood out here. This is just, somehow, my home." He rose from the step. "I'd better unload the car, I guess."

"I've got to sweep out a place to put things. Give me a few minutes. Walk around a little, look around."

He looked at her. "You sure?" The way women got over anything was to get busy doing, just doing.

"Give me a few minutes. You go walk through and make sure there's nothing in there that'll get me and I'll find a place to put things for the night. Tomorrow we can decide how to go about making the place livable. Go ahead, walk around a little. I'll take care of this." She glanced at the car. "There's nothing here I can't handle."

At that he left her to her sense of order and walked down the hallway, leaning to look into the rooms. Filthy, simply filthy, clutter everywhere. And liquor bottles. Liquor bottles and beer cans in every room. He passed on through onto the back porch and down into the back yard, where he shoved a mossy wooden cover off the well and leaned over the ledge. His face was at the center of a silver disk below him. At least there was water, though God only knew what was in it. He'd have to send someone down to clean it out, some boy, if he could find one who would do it. If not, hell, he would go down himself, as he had done once for his grandfather. He walked back around the house and crossed the road.

The main barn seemed solid enough, even after nearly fifty years. He could only vaguely remember his grandfather and father building it, but one image stood out clearly: his father poised on the peak of the bright tin roof crowing like a rooster, his dark hair and sun-reddened face and upper torso sharing a patch of sky with the day moon that hung mysteriously over the woods behind him. He shook the memory from his mind, noting that after all the years and changes of tenants the roof, though sagging slightly, was still in remarkably good shape—he wouldn't know for sure about leaks until it rained. The pens were simply worthless, posts and rails rotted and tilted or fallen, wire rusted, sagging, broken. He would have to replace all that. But he had not expected much more. The small-livestock barn, off to the side, seemed almost unchanged. The roof naturally dipped a bit in the middle, the tin was darker with rust, but everything else looked so familiar that for a brief instant he imagined bumping and bleating and murmuring from the stalls. A sound from the house brought him back.

He turned and looked across the road. His wife, her hair golden in the sun, had thrown out some bottles and was leaning off the back porch shaking a broom or mop. She banged it against the rail and the sound came to him, it seemed, long after she had turned and disappeared into the house. He opened the door of the little barn and stepped inside. It was as he had remembered it, the tiny stalls, low loft, spongy straw floor, but the soft sounds of calves and the mingling odor of urine and milk and sweet feed and hay were gone. He stood a long time in the subdued light and let his mind go back; then, almost as if a hand reached out and drew him to it, he walked to the ladder at the end of the little barn and climbed into the loft. Even as a boy he had had to watch his head as he moved about up there; now he had to slither on his belly to avoid the rough-cut rafters. In the failing light of the late afternoon sun slicing through cracks and knotholes he worked his way into the tight front corner of the loft and slid his hand through layers of old straw until he found the board he was feeling for.

That evening they sat in the middle of a well-scrubbed circle in the kitchen floor before a Coleman lantern, whose sighing and hissing were amazingly loud in the empty house. He had nailed two pieces of tin over the opening where the front door had hung and propped the door to the back porch in place. The back kitchen windows were intact, and she had wedged a piece of cardboard into the frame of the north window, which had probably been knocked out by a rock from the road. There had been two large rocks and half a brick in the pile of trash she had swept from the kitchen. Their belongings were piled neatly on fresh newspapers spread out along the inside wall beside them.

"Maybe tomorrow we can move out of the kitchen," she proposed, wiping from her mouth a trace of ketchup from the burger and fries he had driven over fifteen miles to buy. "I just couldn't manage more than this little clearing for now. Jesus, how dirty!" She shuddered.

"Yeah, like niggers have been living here."

"You can't blame all this mess on them. There's no telling how many different people have stayed in this place since the last family moved out. There's an old mattress upstairs that somebody's been doing something on besides sleeping, judging by the number of condoms in the closet. I'll bet you high school kids use this place like it was theirs."

He grinned. "Maybe we could charge them rent, huh? That'd supplement our income."

"Or at least they could let us watch," she said almost in a whisper.

He stared at her face, which brightened and darkened with the pulsing of the lantern. "Mary Ann, it's not like you to say something like that." My God, what was she coming to? Sometimes he felt like he just didn't know her at all anymore.

She had settled back against the wall, her legs pulled up to her chest the way he had sat on the porch earlier. "Jim, it's been a long time since I've been excited about anything, much less sex. I kneeled down on that mattress . . ."

"And?" Good God, he really *didn't* know her.

She turned her head toward the dark windows. "Nothing. You'll just say it doesn't sound like me."

"I won't, I won't. Tell me." He reached across for her, but she pulled away into the corner of the kitchen, squeezing in between two of their bags.

"No. Let's talk about something else."

"Mary Ann, tell me, please."

"No. Let's discuss something else."

"If that's what you want." He reached a hand out to her and pulled her to her feet. "Let's sit on the steps."

He slid the door aside and they sat on the steps of the back porch watching the moon drift up out of the tree line rimming the hills behind the house. There was much that needed to be said, but little that either wanted to say. He knew how she felt about giving up their house of twelve years and a reasonable life in Houston—whatever reasonable meant—to come back here and do whatever it was they were going to do.

"How'll we ever live?" she had asked him. "How'll we manage without friends? We don't know anybody out there." He had merely told her that she didn't have to come, that it was something *he* had to do and she didn't. "But I am going," he said finally, and refused any further discussion.

And she must have known that he had no answers, that he could no more explain why he had to do it than he could tell her how far it was to the stars that flanked the moon, which he noticed seemed larger and rounder and whiter than he had seen it in years. She had elected to follow—it was her choice.

Life had to be awfully damned confusing for her, maddening. When finally you got to the point where you had probably about figured out where you fit into it all, the rug got jerked out from under you and you found yourself flat on your butt, sitting on the steps of a dilapidated house in the middle of nowhere with all that you owned stashed in a ring around a scrubbed wooden clearing behind you, a man you were almost afraid of beside you, and before you the biggest and brightest moon you had ever seen in your life. She couldn't be anything *but* confused and frightened.

She cleared her throat. "The moon's really bright."

He did not answer, but his arm reached out and pulled her close. His body was warm in the cool October air. Some sort of small birds darted out of the trees and across the moon.

"I used to think," he said after a long while, "lying up there watching that moon come up out of the hills, that there was nothing else but this—this place, these hills and woods, me and my grandparents—knowing full well that my parents were sleeping in a house a hundred miles away, surrounded by other houses and buildings. But everything else seemed remote and strange and unreal, like a dream. The only thing that was really real was all this, just as far as I could see from that bedroom and no farther. There was a—a harmony." He swept his arm in a broad arc. "In the daylight I didn't feel quite that way. Maybe because there was always something to remind me that there was an outside world—a radio going and vapor trails off over the hills, the sounds of sawmills and occasional traffic on the road. At night, though, there was just whatever I could see in that moonlight."

He stood and pulled her to her feet and out away from the house. He pointed to an upstairs window. "From that window right there. Those nights when the moon was out I knew just this world. And it was good, Mary Ann, it was like some sort of Eden, like I was special and somehow the center of Creation, and all this was for me, for my pleasure. Time moved slowly, and I could savor it. And, Mary Ann, through that screen up there every night that the moon was out, it made a cross."

"What do you mean, a cross?"

"You've never seen the moon through screen wire? The light is refracted and thrown along the wires, vertically and horizontally. It makes a little cross."

"No," she said, "I've never seen anything like that."

"God," he sighed, pulling her back to the steps, "God, I loved it." The moon was bright on their faces.

"Is that what you really want to be out here for, then, just to feel like that again?"

"Partly, probably. But it's more complex. I've been places enough now that not even a moon like that can fool me into believing that this is the only world there is. Of course I knew even then, but to believe . . ."

She lightly held his hand.

Much more complex. Too complex to tell. Like living in Houston in a house built on a sea of mud, which flexed and subsided and tossed the foundation so violently over the seasons that cracks formed wide enough to stand a pencil up in. And knowing that even in your most private hours not thirty feet away, beyond walls so flimsy that a car veering off the street could crash through your bedroom and into the den before it met enough resistance to stop, other people were dreaming that they were alone in each other's arms. A child crying in the night two houses down could penetrate your sleep as if he cried in the next room. And the uncertainty of your job, where one year you got a raise and promotion and two years later someone you'd never seen before called you into his office to tell you that because of the collapse of oil prices you'd have only another month with the company. Then the agonizing move from one temporary job to another, your savings steadily diminishing, wife too nervous and hooked on the bottle to augment your income, son's drug treatments siphoning off any extra you did make. A heavy industrial fog lay over everything day after day. And crime, everywhere. And traffic. "It's all clichés," he said to break the silence. "All the reasons."

She cleared her throat. "You wanted to get back to the *real* world? When we start trying to live off this land and whatever interest eighty thousand dollars will generate, we'll know what the real world is."

"At least we've got the eighty thousand dollars."

"We could put that into the house and outbuildings and not have enough left over to even begin to buy equipment and animals." She laughed out loud. "Maybe you've got it figured out how we'll make it, but I'm damned if I can. An open well, and it filthy, no indoor plumbing, no appliances. We don't even know when we can get the electricity turned on."

"Monday," he said. "They promised that they'd turn it on Monday."

She shook her head and pulled her hand away from his. "Nothing to run with it, but we'll have electricity. My God, Jim, don't you see what I'm facing? I've never known this kind of world. I've never spent so much as a night on a farm, and here you are expecting me to be a farm wife right off on a place that can't even be called a farm. I need a drink. Bad."

He stood up and faced her. "Don't talk about drinking, Mary Ann. You swore off it. You swore. And let me remind you that I never made you come out here. You chose to."

"Well, damn, Jim, what were my options? A thirty-seven-year-old alcoholic woman with no job, no skills, no education, no damned money, a house with eight-hundred-dollar-a-month payments. Hey, you never prepared me for something like this. I had to tag along with you or else. What could I do?"

"You could have moved in with your mother."

"Bullshit. Anything but that. I'd rather take real bullshit on my feet every day than endure that kind of hell. That old woman and I would be sprawled out in her living room right now, drunk as the wind, and it'd be that way every night until we both died."

Even in the moonlight he could tell that her face was a blazing red. He reached out to touch her shoulder, but she flung his hand away.

"I spent my life following you—through those awful days out in the Permian Basin, then to Houston, the good days and bad. I tried to raise our child . . ." She choked at that and buried her face in her hands.

"Mary Ann, don't, don't."

"I couldn't even do that on my own. I had to let them take him. Dead at sixteen." Her shoulders heaved. "Oh, Jim, I couldn't even be a mother on my own."

"Mary Ann, get a grip on yourself."

"Dead at sixteen—"

"Mary Ann, that's enough. We've been through all this a thousand times. It's over, done, and we can't get him or those years back. We've lived it and it's over." He sat back down beside her and pulled her into his arms. "There, there."

She quieted then and let him stroke her hair. The moon rose up in its faraway beauty, brightening the pair as they clung to each other while far off, beyond the hills, beyond the moon-emblazoned sky, the darkness hovered.

A car roared by out front, boiling up a dust cloud that slid down the slope toward the woods. Its lights bounced along the road and disappeared over the rise. When quiet returned he suggested that they go in and try to get some sleep. "Tomorrow we'll start cleaning up this place."

"And I can start learning how to be a farm wife," she said drearily.

The door back in place, he pumped the Coleman up and set it on the counter. "Where do you suppose we'd better sleep?"

She shook her head. "I don't know. No bed, no sleeping bags. Sheets and blankets we got. I guess we could just throw out some blankets right here and pad the floor, then put the sheets on and throw blankets over us."

"That floor'll be hard as hell. That's heart-pine." He drove his shoe heel down onto it.

"Stop it. You'll stir up dust. What do you want to do?"

"I don't know. You said something about a mattress upstairs?"

"Jim, that mattress is probably more alive than we are. Those kids have slept and screwed and smoked dope up there. It's filthy."

"We could put down a blanket and sheets."

"I haven't even swept the floor."

"That's OK. Let's take up some stuff and make do. I want to sleep upstairs." He grabbed a garbage bag labeled sheets and handed it to her and shoved a stack of blankets under his arm. He reached for the shotgun leaning in a corner. "We'd better take this." With her right behind him, the lantern thrust in front, they mounted the groaning stairs.

"Those little bastards have been screwing in *my* room." He set the lantern and shotgun down beside the mattress, which was shoved against the inside wall. The floor, he noticed, was almost as clean as the clearing she had made in the kitchen, as if the kids, or whoever they were, had set up housekeeping there. The other rooms were littered with filth—newspapers and paper cups and bags from hamburger joints, liquor bottles, beer cans, old clothes—and everything smelled of urine and age, but here the room had been kept reasonably clean. He glanced at the window and noted that none of the panes were broken, that, in fact, the screen was still there.

"It's almost like they were expecting us," she said. "I didn't notice before how clean it was. I just looked at the mattress."

"Pretty ratty all right. But I guess it served its purpose."

"Look in the closet, Jim." She walked over and swung the door open. "Look here." On the inside of the door someone had driven rows of small finishing nails, dozens of them, and filling out the rows from the top were condoms, hung by their rims.

He stepped back, picked up the lantern, and held it close. "My God, what is this, a trophy case?"

"I don't know. But look—they've been washed out. They look almost like they've never been used."

He leaned forward and blew across one of the rows. "Oh, they've been used all right, but someone has laundered them. Maybe he uses them over and over."

"Monday morning wash, huh? Well, I've never seen anything like it, but I guess we'd better figure out what we're going to do here. Hand me one of the old blankets."

Across the mattress they spread the blanket they had sat on at supper, then added another, then the sheets. When she had tucked under the two cover blankets, she rose and stood back and with a slight bow motioned with her hand: "There is our bed for the night."

"I am impressed," he said, "but let's not go to bed yet." He turned off the lantern and pulled her toward the window, through which the moon streamed. He grasped the window and shoved it up. As they kneeled before the opening a cool drift of October air washed over them. He pointed to the pattern where moonlight broke through the rusty screen. "Look there."

"Yeah. I guess they kept this one up to keep out mosquitoes."

"No, no. The *cross*. Look at the little cross formed by the moon."

She reached out and stroked the screen. "I guess you could call it a cross, the way the light moves both ways at once. It looks vaguely like one. I guess it's a cross. If you say so."

He put his arm around her waist and tried to pull her to him, but she stiffened and drew away. "Mary Ann, you're so stiff. Like you're afraid, like you're getting ready to run from something. What is it?"

She turned to him then and fixed her eyes hard on his face. The moon was so bright on them that there was no mistaking the fury that had risen up to choke off her words. She glared, shuddered, and slid away from him into a corner of the room, where she huddled in darkness like a child as he stared, bathed in moonlight, at the woman who in recent years had been such an enigma.

For long minutes they looked at each other, one out of darkness, one into darkness, while the moon went on in its relentless climb. It was simply no time for words. Far off, deep in the woods along the creek and away in the hills, owls hooted and nightbirds called. A dog or fox barked somewhere, and the shadows of birds twice flitted across the screen.

The longer he stared into the corner at her, the better he could make out what he was seeing: a desperate woman snatched from a world she had a tenuous hold on and dumped into one that she knew *nothing* of. This was not for her what it was for him, his moon no more to her than a streetlight and his woods and hills as alien as a distant star, and if he saw a cross of moonlight in the screen how could he assume that she must see one too? No longer young, but not old either, not yet, that woman huddled in the darkness of the room was still the delicate thing he had courted and coaxed and married and loved deeply for a dozen years before the fetid world of outer darkness, somewhere beyond the moonlit world that he now knew was indeed the only one he could be happy in, had collapsed on them as he suspected all along that it someday would, scarring and souring her so that he might never really touch her again.

She crouched deep in the corner, knees drawn into her chest, head clasped in her hands, staring out at him until the moonlight had inched almost to her feet. The closet door still stood open, the condoms lightly rippling in the breeze from the window.

She broke the silence first. "They look like little ghosts." She pointed toward the condoms.

He turned and looked. In the moonlight reflected off the floor the condoms glowed. "They do. They do look like little ghosts," he whispered.

"I'm coming out of the corner now. I'm over it." She crawled up beside him. "I was just feeling sorry for myself. I'm sorry." She leaned and kissed him on the cheek. "I can't promise that I won't have more problems coming to terms with life out here, but I'll try to hang on. I'll try to see a cross when you see a cross." Then she added, "And I'll try to bear it the best I can."

"That was clever," he said, holding her. "And it was clever to say that the rubbers look like ghosts."

"Not really. That's what they do look like, like little Caspers hanging upside down." She pointed to the screen. "And I really can see a cross."

He laughed out loud at that. "I wonder how he'll take it, the kid whose love nest we've taken over?"

"I don't know," she answered. "What if he comes back for his laundry?"

"Mary Ann." He had pulled from his shirt pocket a clutch of folded pages. "Look at this." He carefully unfolded the sheets and spread them out on the moonlit floor. They were age-dimmed pictures of women in very old-style underwear, girdles and panties that rose past the navel, brassieres large and stiff-looking and formidable.

"What *are* they?"

"I dug them out this afternoon, from the loft of the small barn. Just a whim. I put them there when I was a little boy, probably twelve or so."

"But what *are* they? What are they from?"

He was grateful that in the subdued light his face would not show the full blush that he felt. "They're from a Sears catalog, God knows what date. I tore them out of one that my grandmother was throwing away. I did that every time I found one that she was going to put in the barrel to burn." He ran his hand softly across the women's bodies. "They were my women. I used to stare at them for hours trying to imagine what they would look like without their panties and bras."

"My God, Jim, you were using the Sears catalog as porn?"

"Light porn, my dear, very light, but the closest thing to *Playboy* that I ever got my hands on out here."

"And you remembered hiding them out there?"

"Yeah, just like I did it yesterday. The wonder is that they have lasted all this time. I wrapped them in waxed paper—that saved them. They're a little yellowed, but other than that they look about the same." He held the sheets up and kissed one of the women. "My girls, my women."

"Old women now—not even waxed paper could have saved the real ones."

He carefully folded the pages and returned them to his pocket. "Tomorrow I'll put them back where they belong, in retirement. God, how fascinating to imagine where they are right now, the real women in these pictures, who they've loved and been loved by, what they look like now, what lives they've had. I wonder if any of them ever thought about the boys who drooled over them. How sad."

She nodded, squeezing his hand.

"When I'm an old man," he said, "I'll take them out again and we can look at them in the moonlight." He cleared his throat. "I don't really need them anymore—I've got my own real-life woman, who wears bikini panties and goes as often without a bra as with one."

"Waxed paper wouldn't have helped her much either."

"Well, it's been tough the last few years, what with Donald and—"

"And the bottle," she added.

"Yes. That didn't help."

"But no more. I promised and I'll stick to it." This time *she* reached out, slipping her arms around him and clasping him to her. "I don't know how I'll fare out here, but I'm willing to give it a heroic try. Maybe after we get electricity and appliances and indoor plumbing—and indoor plumbing had better come quick, because I hate using that outhouse . . ."

"And kids."

"Kids?"

"Kids. My great-grandmother didn't stop having kids until she was over forty-five—you've got nearly ten years of childbearing left in you. Wouldn't it be fine to raise two or three kids out here?"

But she had stopped listening and talking. Tears shone on her face.

What an absurd notion, he realized, suggesting having children at her age, having children way the hell out here. What a joke, what an incredibly crazy joke. He wasn't sure what the tears were from—fear, laughter, uncertainty, grief, maybe all of them—but he had them too.

He wasn't sure what either of them was feeling, but he knew that in the moonlight his woman hadn't changed that much at all, that she was just as pretty and young-looking as ever, and that he wanted her, really wanted her, for the first time in years. He pulled her face to his and kissed her, almost violently, and began unbuttoning her shirt.

Tomorrow would be soon enough to talk about plumbing, electricity, and having children. Now what mattered was that a man and woman lay down gently together and they and forest and field and all Creation beneath the rising moon, all the world that they were certain existed, all pulsed in a harmony as ancient as the rock-ribbed hills surrounding them.

THE
SURVIVALIST

T H E night of his fifty-seventh birthday Harley Simmons lay on his mattress staring at the ceiling of the basement, where leaks from upstairs, from the roof or plumbing—he didn't know and didn't care which—had stained the sheetrock, making arabesque shapes that he imagined sometimes were dark angels, at others outright devils. Beside him on a table made of a mortar-shell crate a candle burned, stood upright in a loaf of canned nutbread, and a half-empty bottle of survival whiskey weaved beside the candle. It was late, the television was dead, and his war map wavered faintly in the glow of the flame. In his right hand, which lay across his chest as if in solemn pledge, Harley held his heavy service automatic, the hammer cocked.

For decades Harley had nurtured an apocalyptic vision that one day the world would lose its pinnings and tumble into chaos, leaving only the strong and well-prepared to savor deliverance, calculate the damage, and start things over.

Almost without exception the catastrophe took the form of global nuclear war: He would be routinely walking his route, one hand clutching a clump of letters, the other holding his can of

Mace (precaution against sudden attack by dogs), when a woman would burst through the door he was approaching and scream that inbound Russian missiles would be landing in half an hour. With letters still drifting back to earth like pieces of sky falling on the lady's lawn, he would rush to his jeep and in less than fifteen minutes be carefully initiating his survival procedures while his wife looked on, horrified, her hands rolled in a hard ball in her apron front, frozen with a fear such as she had never known.

Sometimes, though, there would be a race war with blacks and Hispanics and whites battling each other through the streets, neither local law nor national guard nor federal troops able to restore order. Those dreams almost always came as he walked his route of just over four blocks through part of the Negro section of town. Black masses poured down from Dallas, brown hordes surged up from Houston, and every small town between the two waves fell victim to their pillaging and torture and rape. These dreams ended with him laying volleys of rifle and shotgun fire across the advancing dark ranks of the enemy while his neighbors' houses burned.

A less frequent disaster was economic collapse of the country, with the poor—black, brown, and white—rampaging through the cities and towns; starving and violent beyond belief, they roared over the landscape like a great prairie fire, leaving nothing but smoldering ruins in their wake. Only here and there a house still stood among the rubble and bodies of the dead, formidable and defiant, a fortress with food and water and weapons, able to survive for a year, if need be, before order came again.

Invasion by foreign powers occupied little of his dream time, but once while he was fishing with a friend in the Valley a vivid scenario developed: Mammoth armies of Central Americans and Mexicans, trained and led by Russians and Cubans, boiled up across Texas and fanned out over the entire southern half of the country, establishing a front line that ran from central California to Virginia. Americans who remained behind the line, the few hundred thousand brave souls who survived the initial onslaught by whatever manner of luck and skill, did so at great peril. Each day bands of marauding aliens, more often lawless rabble than actual troops, took to the streets to murder any Americans they encountered and scavenge for spoils of war. Occasionally there was a house they would not approach, the bodies of their dead heaped in a festering ring about it to declare the beginning of a zone of death. Even the military authorities, busy enough with the war along the front, avoided such fortresses, preferring simply to allow them their sovereignty until civil government could be allowed to rule again.

A few times he had tried other approaches to the apocalypse, exercising all manner of natural disasters from meteor strikes to gargantuan hurricanes, but none of these played out to his satisfaction, principally because, though each wrought great ruin upon the earth, none gave him much opportunity to bring his wits and weapons to bear against an actual enemy.

The nuclear-war scenario pleased him most and pervaded both his sleeping and waking dreams. It had, after all, the promise of combining the threats of all the others, with the added dimensions of radiation and nuclear winter. Certainly there was the possibility, even probability, of economic collapse, race wars, and invasion, with targets enough to make the last days interesting.

It was not something he talked about, not even with close friends, among whom he could name only three at most: two fellow workers and a plumbing contractor who lived on the street behind him. He was out with them—drinking, fishing, or hunting—perhaps a dozen times a year. A private person, he preferred the company of his wife most of the time; besides, anyone with a dream of Armageddon naturally wanted to stay close to home.

"We don't ever go anywhere," his wife said to him one evening after a month of tensions in the Middle East had kept him before the television every waking hour when he wasn't delivering mail.

"Why should we? What could be more interesting than what's going on over there? The fate of the world could be sealed right there in five minutes if something went wrong." He pointed to the set. "With Russians all over and our Persian Gulf fleet and Iranians and Iraqians with planes and gunboats and tanks running around shooting at anything that flies or floats or crawls, anything could happen. I want to know about it when it does."

"Why? What could you do about it, Harley?" She was sitting beside him on the couch folding underwear from the dryer.

He moved away from the pile of hot underwear. "I could—well, I don't know exactly what I could do, but whatever happened, you and me would be all right."

He knew that talking about it with her would go nowhere. It never had. She humored him, and that was enough. If he asked her to buy another case of Spam at the store, she did, and he dated it and added it to the cases of canned meats and fruit and vegetables and gallons of bottled water and cases of Coke stacked along the walls of the basement. She never complained about the dozens of guns he had hidden all over the house; and though once she worried out loud to him about the explosion hazard of the thousands of rounds of ammunition and cans of gunpowder in a cabinet in the basement, she had said nothing since.

She knew how he felt about being prepared. He had explained to her on countless occasions what the world could come to in less than half an hour, how civilization could lapse overnight into the Dark Ages, leaving only the strong and prepared and those who would take away what they had so carefully preserved.

"Did you know," he asked her as they watched CNN news the day the U.S. shot down two Libyan jets, "that in the aftermath of a nuclear war the biggest element of barter would be .22 ammunition?" She shook her head. "Think of the number of people in this country with .22's, and they'll all be needing bullets for hunting and home defense and there won't be any but what people have laid aside. A .22 bullet would be worth its weight in gold." She smiled. "And, Madge," he continued, "I got eighty-seven pounds of that stuff in the basement."

He knew, though again it was not something he would ever really talk to people about, that if things got bad enough a case of Spam could be traded for a car or a house. Hell, people would be killing over cans of meat and jugs of water. If the nuclear winter notion did check out, his hoard of rice and canned goods and flour would not only sustain him and his wife, but through shrewd trading he could come out of the chaos an extremely wealthy man.

As each crisis sparked, developed, and resolved itself, he became increasingly convinced that the world could not hold together much longer. Only a hair's breadth away from disaster each time, only that: One slip of the thumb, one irrational command, one confused message, and his finest hour would begin.

He had missed the wars. Too young for WWII and kept out of the Asian wars by a bad back, he had always been denied the opportunity for heroism. He had not even been mugged, never had to fire on an intruder, never been called on to save a lovely woman from rape. One night after watching a tape of *Death Wish* with Madge, he slipped out of the house late and, quite drunk, drove to Houston and walked alone through the roughest neighborhood he could find, a service automatic wedged beneath his belt—but nothing came of it, no one even seemed to notice he was there, and he dragged back in just before dawn, a weary and disappointed man.

With all his guns and thousands of rounds of ammunition, he had never come close to firing a shot at anyone, though he often recalled the night he had heard a noise in his garage and came within a wink of sending a charge of buckshot through one of his wife's robes hanging on a nail. All his shooting, and there had been plenty of it, was at silhouettes on the range.

"All I really want," he told his wife one evening as they were settling down to sleep, "is what most men want—the chance to prove that under fire I am worth my salt. Here I am getting old, Madge, and each day that I live I am that much farther from doing something heroic. I'd just like to see what I'm really made of—you know, what kind of spine I really got. You know, like Churchill or MacArthur or, hell, even Hitler."

She patted him on the back. "You are a good husband, Harley, and I am proud of you. I just wish you wouldn't worry so much about nuclear wars and such. It's not healthy."

"Madge," he said quietly, "I'm not worried that one will happen—I'm worried that one *won't*."

She gasped in the dark. "Only a man that doesn't have a wife or anyone or anything else to live for would say that. It looks like to me that you are getting a bad case of the nerves." He talked with her less and less about his obsession after that. It was a stupid thing to have said, he would admit, but it was the way he felt. He much preferred a cataclysm with fire and smoke and bombs and bullets to the gradual grinding down of life to a pitiful puddle of flesh. He'd seen too much of that: his father, his wife's father, two aunts, sundry people he knew or had heard of, worn down by living until, merely shells, they passed out of this life more helpless than they came into it. He couldn't bear thinking of his life ending that way.

"Besides," he said to himself one morning as he stared into the bathroom mirror before shaving, "it is not unhealthy to anticipate something that in all probability is going to happen. Hell, we worry about little stuff all the time, petty things that in a few days or weeks are usually resolved, one way or another, so where's the harm in thinking about the biggest worry of all? Lord, there never was a greater worry." He patted his sagging belly and grimaced at the balding little man that looked back at him.

Born a few years before the outbreak of World War II, he could recall precisely, though he was only a boy, the instant he first heard about the atomic bomb. He was staying at his grandparents' house with his mother while his father was away in Europe. One morning, only a few weeks before his father was due home, an uncle, just back from Europe himself and still wearing his khaki uniform, burst through the door waving a newspaper and shouting, "We have dropped the atom bomb on the Japs."

So it was that Harley Simmons was introduced to The Bomb and became a child of the nuclear age. From that morning in 1945 he knew that someday the dark angels of evil would clash with the good and that out of the rubble under the blank skies of that Armageddon would rise men of courage and strength not seen in centuries.

Though he did indeed have recurring dreams about nuclear war—as was only natural, given the nervousness of the world

during the fifties, with talk of bomb shelters and such—his notion of preparing for the apocalypse did not come to him until
just after the Cuban missile crisis, when, as a young mail carrier
with a pregnant wife, he had watched mesmerized as events developed that could have taken the world over the proverbial
brink. He and Madge had sat before the television for hours
as tensions built, and they both believed that the stress of the
crisis was in large part to blame for the miscarriage that came
shortly after.

As the world subsided into its routine in the aftermath of the
superpower standoff, for months Harley had felt cheated. It was
as if after rising to the point of some final glorious battle the two
countries had backed off like tired old men afraid of striking a
blow. Emotionally drained by the missile crisis and Madge's miscarriage, he spent the next year trying to get a focus on his life
again, while boredom settled on his spirits day after day as palpable as dust. Life at home was a merciless hollow dialogue with
Madge or endless television, even his woodworking shop offering
little respite, and his job was a mechanical regimen better suited
to a robot that could scan addresses and zip door to door with
the mail.

One day while he was working his route near the noon hour,
he decided to pull into a little neighborhood park and have his
lunch, a simple sandwich and fried pie, packed by Madge that
morning. As was his custom, he stayed in the jeep, his eye on the
stacks as he ate; and as was also his custom, he fingered through
the mail for a magazine to read during the break. What his eyes
stopped on was not a magazine but a brochure with the stark
white title *Surviving* imposed on a background of bombed buildings, piles of skeletons, and a sky black with a cloud of smoke that
had been drawn to resemble a huge grinning skull. Before his
lunch hour was over he had read the little publication twice and
jotted down the address of the publisher. Thus began Harley Simmons's life as a survivalist.

From the little brochure and subsequent publications from a
survivalist press in Louisiana he learned not only that there would
be survivors of a nuclear war but that there would be millions and

those who did survive would face an even greater enemy than the Russians in defending themselves and their family and property from the starving throngs who would seize everything in their path. One newsletter was devoted almost exclusively to outlining steps a homeowner could take to prepare himself for the world after Armageddon: stockpiling supplies, manufacturing medicines, accumulating weapons and ammunition, securing property against fallout, and later fending off assault by masses of hungry poor—the advice went on and on, and with each issue Harley's interest in surviving grew.

From the beginning he prepared feverishly, realizing that if the war came on them suddenly he and Madge would be ill-suited to make a go of it in the rubble. The very day after his first copy of *The Survivalist's Newsletter* arrived, he went with Madge to the grocery store and, over her protests, bought a case of Spam and eight jugs of purified water.

She stood beside him as he loaded the groceries in the car. "I do not know what's going on with you, Harley, but we could not eat that much Spam in a year, and what's all this bottled water for?"

On the way home he explained to her what the newsletter had said about canned meat and bottled water being the key ingredients in any home's survival store, and he insisted that over the next few months she was to add ten jugs of water and a case of Spam each week until they had a hundred gallons of water and ten cases of Spam stacked in the basement. "After we get that done, I'll list other stuff I want you to get." She shook her head and sat in silence.

He had never been a hunter, had not, in fact, even owned a gun, except for one of his grandfather's old shotguns, which he was not certain was safe to fire. The newsletter stressed a range of firearms for home defense, so he set about stocking his arsenal: whether near or far, many or few, armored or not, the enemy could be dealt with. For long-range, carefully aimed shots, he chose a scoped bolt-action Remington, whose 7-mm magnum bullet would travel flat and true for three hundred yards and drop a man built like a moose; for massed enemy at great range he purchased a surplus M-1, not for its accuracy but for its eight-round charge of ammunition. For close-in defense he went with two pump-action shotguns, a .45 automatic pistol, and two revolvers. He added a .22 pistol and rifle for hunting and bought for Madge a snub-nosed .38, which she refused even to look at.

In spite of Madge's spirited objections he took out a moderate loan at the bank to finance his preparedness. The price of security was always high, he told her—hell, anyone in government could tell you that. When it was done, though, when over the years he finally had his basement stocked the way it should be, he knew that no matter what awful fate befell the world, he and Madge would survive. They had over a hundred jugs of water, cases of colas, rice, beans, canned vegetables and meat, dried fruits, two brimming freezers, a generator with six 55-gallon drums of gasoline, and reloading supplies to replenish the thousands of rounds of ammunition, should they be expended. A surveillance system notified them when anyone entered the driveway, and switches and electronic eyes lay ready to signal any intrusion of the house. The only thing he could figure that they really needed to complete their preparation was a bomb shelter, but every time he brought the issue up Madge said that she would go home to her mother by nightfall the day he had one delivered.

The home of Harley and Madge Simmons, then, became a bastion against whatever sinister forces might lie dormant, waiting for a chance to rise out of the rubble of nuclear devastation like fierce black angels that would sweep over the landscape slashing and slaughtering anything in their path. And so it remained over the years as crisis after crisis blossomed and faded, each bringing the world right to the brink of war, then disappearing, only to bloom again, as perpetual as spring. On the world map that covered half of one wall of his basement Harley plotted the development of each crisis until the great rectangle was dotted with red circles, some small, some large. "And some day," he often said to himself as he made another circle and studied its position and potential for growth, "I will draw a red circle around all of it."

Secure only in their home, they ventured out seldom, he to work, she to do whatever shopping needed to be done; they ate out only once or twice a year, on special occasions, and then in the little East Texas town they lived in. Never much for traveling, they spent their weekends and vacations with reading and television, some piddling around the house, more television. Their days began with CNN news and the papers, waxed into television game shows and midday news, then slid into afternoons of tedium—usually soap operas—and peaked with the evening news, when invariably commentators turned to the Middle East or Central America and mounting tensions between the superpowers. Harley's weekdays were broken up by his eight-hour shifts with the mail.

Madge had become decidedly less communicative as the years passed, going about her housework like a zombie, sitting with a magazine or newspaper or watching television for hours without looking up or aside or speaking. Harley took it as an indication that her mind was going, along with her body, which, he noticed more and more frequently, had burgeoned into a shape that twenty years before she would have laughed at anyone else for having. Her mother was dying in a distant hospital, a fact that surely troubled her, but he would under no circumstances entertain the notion of a trip to Virginia with world tensions the way they were, and she would not go without him. A sad, silent woman, she moved through the house and his life like a shadow.

Neither of them had siblings, and whatever friends they had known over the years gradually drifted away, doubtless spooked by Harley's morose silence and social alienation. He no longer hunted or fished or drank with anyone, and if he happened to come within earshot of his plumber neighbor, they merely said hello and went busily on their way. He had little to say to anyone at the post office or on his route—he did his job and went home, the only place he felt comfortable anymore. If people did not understand, the problem was theirs: Someday it would all make sense, but it would be too late for them.

Harley allowed himself few diversions from his job and the monitoring of world affairs, but one Saturday each month he drove to the local range and fired two or three of his weapons. Madge steadfastly refused to go with him. He had replaced his old M-1 with an AR-15, the civilian version of the army's M-16, which used a clip of twenty or thirty rounds, making it a far more effective weapon against mass assaults. Lining up a dozen or so human silhouettes at the two-hundred-yard line, he would pretend that they were the dark hordes from Houston and blaze away with the rifle until all hung tattered on their chicken-wire backings. Another option was to hang the targets at twenty-five or fifty yards and shred them with a shotgun or volley after volley of pistol rounds. In time he became so incredibly decisive with his shooting that he knew it would take an entire company of well-armed infantry to seize his house. After his sessions at the range, he picked up every round of empty brass and pocketed it for reloading.

After the evening news, when others played with their kids or enjoyed poker or bridge or lolled about in the bars, Harley religiously loaded round after round of ammunition at his workbench or studied his world charts or inventoried his supplies while Madge lay inert before the television until sleep took her, sometimes so completely that she slept on the couch through the night. Harley always made the ten o'clock news, then went back either to the basement or to bed, after first having made his security check, a matter simply of determining that all the doors were locked and the burglar alarm armed and glancing out through each window to be certain that no strange shadows moved on the lawn.

It was the year that Harley made his decision to take early retirement—his back had gotten worse, joined by ailing feet—that Madge halted midstride with a load of towels she was carrying to the washer and fell among them in a great heap, where he found her when he came in that day, dead as the basement floor she landed on. Her heart, the doctor said, though Harley told the few people who attended the funeral and visited him briefly afterwards that he believed that Madge simply grew tired of life and willed herself out of it. "Life didn't have enough excitement for her," he confided in a letter to her mother, who herself died a month later.

Harley handled Madge's death well at first. Life had not been easy in her years of decline, and it was almost with relief that he came home to the empty house after a day on the route. He continued using the kitchen and bathroom and bedroom, and he watched television from the couch they had shared. Weekends he even ventured into the yard, mowing, trimming, planting shrubs. Neighbors he had seen only in passing to and from work waved over fences at him, smiled, and for one short season Harley Simmons felt like a total human being, glad to be in the sun again.

But Madge had, after all, been the only companion in his fortress against the world and, willingly or not, the one participant in his apocalyptic vision, so in a short while he came to miss her so dreadfully that he vacated the main floor of the house altogether, preferring the familiarity of the basement. He wrestled the television downstairs and positioned it beneath his war map so that all he had to do while watching the news was glance from set to map to see exactly where the day's hotspot was. Then came the refrigerator and range and the mattress from their bed, which served to pad him from the concrete floor.

Within less than half a year after Madge's death, weeds took over the lawn, front and back, and neighbors looked across at a boarded-up house, inside which Harley had even sealed off the door from the kitchen. The basement became his home.

His job, which immediately after Madge's death Harley had come almost to enjoy again, lost all its appeal and became a dreaded weekday sentence that he served grudgingly until the year was out. Then he took his retirement. Setting up his finances so that he could conduct all his worldly affairs from the security of his bunker home, he ventured out less and less. The mailman picked up and delivered mail from a gallon bucket hung at the back door, the garbage men emptied a can set just outside; the only other persons he allowed access to the premises were the utility meter readers and the Negro boy who came by once every month and mowed down the weeds well enough to keep the neighbors from calling and complaining; Harley watched each time as the boy walked past the back window and stooped to pick up the ten-dollar bill that stuck out from beneath the door.

And so it was that on the night of his fifty-seventh birthday Harley Simmons lay alone in his basement bastion studying the ceiling above his head, a dazed, drunk, and disappointed man. His war map graphically chronicled the recent desert war, in which he had felt certain Iraq and Israel would lob nuclear weapons at each other and bring on Armageddon—in fact the war had been a field exercise for American forces and was over in a matter of days. The Eastern Bloc now dissolute, Germany reunited, and the Russian Empire sterile and crumbling, there just didn't seem to be any real need for survivalists anymore. There wasn't anything to survive *from*.

He had dozed off, the unaccustomed whiskey wrapping him like a warm blanket, and awakened with a start at some noise. Pistol in hand, he rolled up on an elbow and listened, but there was nothing outside but the wind, and nothing inside that could have made the sound. His eyes moved from the door back to the stained ceiling to his war map, across which the world stretched peaceful in the twilight of his candle.

He lay flat on the mattress and stared at the ceiling until, the candle burning low, a strange comfort settled on him and he began to see shapes come that he had not seen since he was a child. He raised the pistol to his head. About him crates of survival goods rose like towering buildings of a great silent city, lit only by the flickering of a distant fire, and above the city, their wings wide against the darkening sky, two vast pale angels hovered.

A week later two of Harley's neighbors stood at the edge of their street watching the parade of vehicles that stretched almost beyond sight in both directions, with a clamorous clumping in front of the boarded-up Simmons house. There, along the driveway and out onto the overgrown lawn, were stacks and stacks of canned meat and vegetables, cases of Coke and bottled water. "That's enough provisions to keep an army going," one neighbor said to the other.

There were beds and tables and couches and chairs, appliances and kitchen utensils, tables of guns and ammunition and reloading equipment, generators and tools. "Hell of a sale, I'd say," the other neighbor replied. "Look at him go."

He pointed to a small, balding man who flitted in and among the rummaging people like a liberated bird, answering a question here, holding up an item there, taking money with both hands and stuffing it into his bulging pockets, glancing now and then at the new Winnebago parked under a tree across the lawn.

"You reckon we ought to go on over?" one of them asked.

"Yeah, I 'spect so. Before Harley's sold it all."

The two of them checked their billfolds for cash and started across the street, dodging traffic.

GRIEF

T H E sun, long since out of the backdrop of pines, was already midmorning high when Barbara parked her car and walked to the grave site. There was an order, a saneness about things when the sun was on them, even headstones and monuments beneath which rested the forever dead, even the raw rectangular hole that lay before her. The cemetery was hers. There was no noise, save the clatter of crows off in the pines and the distant hum of Saturday morning traffic, and whoever had dug the hole and erected the crisp green awning had taken their tools and left.

In town the church would be filling soon. Amos would be the centerpiece, his casket lid propped open for the parade of mourners—family, friends, the long train of those whose lives he had touched, and those who had only heard of him but felt compelled to make a final deferential gesture toward the man and legend that Amos Petroski had been. The pews would be packed with whites, who would manage their grief, however genuine, in a careful funereal manner, practiced and restrained, wiping away an occasional tear, and at the rear, along the wall and foyer, the Negroes would stand, polite but noisy in the bereavement so characteristic of the darker races. Each would do his little part to flesh out the drama until the lid was closed on Amos for good.

There was no reason why genuine grief could not be private and silent and dignified and still be real. Her shadow crept from the edge of the hole as the sun rose higher; it stayed just out of reach of the awning shade. She knew how the church would look and smell and feel, with its ritual of flowers and black ribbons, the preponderance of dark clothes, the solemn faces with their painted-on grief. An almost palpable sanctity would pervade the congregation, sliding under clothes, then along bare skin, penetrating finally to the bone. But that was not grief—that was atmosphere created by the music and the minister's voice in the cavernous auditorium, the coughing and sniffling, the frightful carrying on of the Negroes at the rear. *Grief comes from the bone out, it moves like blood, it moves from inside out, not from outside in. I will have no part of their kind of sorrow.* She knelt and looked into the dark hole, where water had already welled up. Her shadow drew slowly back into itself.

Amos, Amos, such a dear man. Too old for her to love like a lover, too young to be a grandfather to her, he lay somewhere in that gray in-between where what she felt for him was neither certain nor particularly strong, but there, always there. He had been her landlord for eighteen years—pleasant, agreeable, ever eager to answer her complaints, almost never increasing the rent (and when he did raise it, the increases were modest and justified by rising taxes or utility rates). It was on his recommendation, she was sure, that she had been hired at the local college back when, with a fresh master's degree in hand, she had little going for her, not even especially good looks. Amos had immediately taken to her, taught her the town, offered her a place to stay at a reasonable price. And in the years that followed, he was always there when she needed a confidant, an adviser, or simply another human voice.

And especially in recent years, as age began to make its mark on her and the finality of her celibate state settled in like the fear of death itself, she had valued Amos's friendship. He had come to her many an evening, knocking lightly until she heard him and let him in and they sat and talked long into the night about things that mattered to them both. So many times, in the deep hours of night she would hear him at the door or dream she had heard him and open the door, only to find no one in the hall. He had never ventured so much as a touching of hands, this pleasant man who now lay lifeless, but he had always been there when she needed him most. Somehow he always knew.

Amos Petroski was a man loved by a county, first as the sheriff, a post he held longer than anyone in Walker County before or after him, then as county judge, a position he occupied right up to the moment of his death, when, like some old warrior weary of his armor and a lifetime of battle, he slumped onto his time-worn judge's desk before astonished attorneys and jury and accused and his gavel came down for the last time.

He was a man neither tall nor handsome nor eloquent of speech; he looked, moved, and spoke like someone's grandfather, even when Barbara had first known him, when he was no older than she was now. It wasn't what he looked like or sounded like that drew people inexorably to him, but what he was. The poor loved him, the wealthy trusted him; even the blacks, who traditionally suspected and dreaded local law, loved and trusted him. No man came to his court fearing injustice and no man left feeling that he had received anything more or less than what God Almighty would have meted out.

But it was not simply the justice of Amos's office as sheriff or county judge that endeared him to these people. It was his willingness, no matter the day or hour, to answer an injustice or respond to an appeal for aid. If some Negro farmer came diffidently to the rear door of the apartment complex on a Sunday morning and, with hat in hand and eyes downcast, mentioned to Amos that so-and-so had not paid his milk bill in a month, Amos would likely as not skip church and even Sunday lunch and drive the farmer out to a distant corner of the county to so-and-so's house. There he would swing down out of his old pickup and confront the arrears milk-consumer with the milk-producer's charge, saying simply and without threat of gavel or badge, "Now, John, you know that an economy works only when one man produces and sells and the other man buys and consumes. You have consumed but not bought, which you and me and Earl here knows ain't right and upsets the whole economy. If a bunch of people did this, the whole county and country would collapse by morning, and don't none of us want that. Now, me and Earl are gon' get back in the truck and give you a few minutes to think this out. When you have come to what you know is the proper decision, when you have looked at this from all angles and come up with what you know's right for all concerned, you come over and tell us about it." Invariably the offender would make things right with himself and in a moment of truth as self-cleansing as revival salvation ask Amos and the man he'd offended to forgive him for his transgressions. Just being around Amos brought out the truth in people. That was the way he was.

When the attack came, it was mercifully quick and certain, striking Amos just as he had passed sentence on Charlie Yates for the theft of two calves and started down with the gavel. The gavel and Amos's head struck the desk at the same time, a great thunk that shook the whole county and reverberated for three days as the word went out: Amos Petroski is dead.

It was three days of agitation of soul for Barbara. She dismissed her history classes, unable to steady herself enough to lecture, and retreated to her apartment. Lying on her couch or across the bed or sitting in the shade-drawn study, she could think of nothing but Amos; her eyes lingered on the many small gifts from him that sat on tables and hung from walls. A phone would jangle somewhere in the complex or the main hall bell would ring, bringing her back to the moment, but she would lose herself again when her eyes returned to the photographs of birds and flowers, forests, fields, to the clumps of dried flowers or marvelously grotesque natural shapes of stone—all gifts from Amos over the years, all witness to his understanding of the real and beautiful. Even the random photographs of blacks and poor whites, which she had accepted even while advising him that she cared nothing for their world, seemed to draw her attention the way they never had. All this from him, from a man who had never touched her.

It was expected, of course, that Barbara would attend the funeral service. Amos's widow called on her, drifting from the doorway to the couch, where like a black dress with no flesh in it she crumpled; she spoke softly of their loss and advised that it had been arranged for Barbara to sit with the family. "It is," she said in rising to go, "as Amos would have wanted it." She looked about the room before closing the door. "It is strange that in all these years with us I have never seen the inside of your apartment. It reminds me terribly of Amos."

The morning of the funeral Barbara dressed hours early, even before first light, and, not fully understanding why, turned away from town and drove out into the country, taking one farm-to-market road, then another, weaving her way back into the areas that had changed but little, she knew, since the first families had settled East Texas and staked out their claims, setting plow to the soil and fencing in the land for livestock. She passed farmers in overalls, some walking from barn to house, others already plowing in the fields, some on horses, some afoot. Though most had tractors, she knew that mules were still used and that if she drove long enough she would see off in a field somewhere a man following an old brown beast in a scene that could have come right out of a past century.

There was little enough change in evidence anyway. The old houses looked like the ones she had seen in Amos's photographs—tin roofs, unpainted boards, porches across the front—and the people living in them, though of the latter twentieth century and wearing permanent-press clothing and driving cars whose shapes looked familiar, seemed more suited to old photographs than real life. The farther she drove, the more she seemed to go back in time. *I am glad I am doing this, but I do not know why I am glad.* She came finally, after following a paved road until it turned into gravel and narrowed and became little more than a field road, to a Negro farm where a crowd of people had gathered. A funeral? This early? What then? She slowed, stopped, and backed up. The people were clustered between the house and barn around sawhorses with boards across them; fires were going, and steam rose in great billows from open iron pots. Then she saw the scaffold: three stark poles tied at the top and spread at the bottom to form a tepee shape. She sat and watched. She was directly across a shallow ditch from the crowd and not a hundred feet from the scaffold. No one looked over at her. Each seemed to have a particular job, the men rolling a barrel and digging a hole, a few standing off near the barn looking into a pen, the women tending the fires and positioning pots and pans on the crude tables. There was no apparent hurry in what they were doing. As Barbara blinked her eyes in deliberate, slow blinks, the frames looked like individual photographs, one little changed from the next. A soft murmur of voices drifted across from the crowd in the sharp morning air.

Someone walked from the house with a gun and handed it to an old man looking over into the pen. He leaned and took aim and Barbara heard the sound of the rifle, a flat snap like an old bone breaking. A roar went up from the crowd and the scene changed from bucolic indolence to the feverish roil of men driven by fire and the sight of blood.

She looked at her watch—early yet—and readjusted her hat and veil in the mirror. She reached to start the car, hesitated. *Why am I doing this? I know what they are doing. Why don't I just go on?* She stared at her eyes in the mirror, then looked back at the crowd, the scaffold.

Now the pig was hanging inverted, a pale blister of flesh, while men scraped hair from it. It was obscenely white, like something that had been kept from the sun, like the underside of something that lived in water or beneath the earth. She watched as, almost in slow motion, an arm tipped with a long bright knife rose from the knot of men about the hog and fell from the juncture of the back legs to the chest. The hog burst open—she thought she could hear it rip—and, as a low throaty sound rose from the people gathered about it, an avalanche of organs and blood fell.

Barbara swallowed the scalding sourness rising in her throat and turned away from the scene, straightened her hat and veil, and pointed her car toward town. *This is not my world. I do not know this world, these people. This is blood and violence, the heart of darkness, and I do not know it.* She leaned her chin on the steering wheel as she drove and looked up toward the deepening sky where stars had been minutes earlier, where satellites carrying on the business of the world were whizzing along in the sun, far from that enclave of the Dark Ages she was running from. "And these," she found herself saying as the car softened onto asphalt, "are the people Amos knew and loved."

A blue and white police car turned into the long cemetery drive; behind it an interminable train of cars and trucks, lights burning, inched through the entrance columns. Barbara rose to her feet and moved back among the nearby headstones, selecting a seat on a concrete boundary that surrounded a large plot within easy sight of the grave. She watched as the funeral line moved solemnly up the drive, closed ranks, and stopped. The line broke at the cemetery entrance and a second string of cars, older and more battered than those that first arrived, eased along the opposite side of the drive. Some cars, she could see through gaps in the shrubbery, stopped at the edge of the street. At last the hearse came in, led and followed by Sheriff's Department cars; it crept between the lines of people on either side of the drive and turned up the narrow lane that led to the grave. The flood of people fell into its wake and upon reaching the awning separated into groups of mourners. The family were seated in folding chairs before the grave and behind them an array of well-dressed white people jostled for position. The poorer whites, conspicuous in their cheaper clothing, stood farther behind. On the other side of the awning, facing into the sun, were the Negroes. As numerous as the whites, they looked like one vast lump of dark primordial flesh, and even now, before any official voice had begun, a collective moan rose from them, the same low, guttural sound she had heard earlier when the hog's stomach fell open and his insides tumbled out. She felt her throat tightening. The whites stood and sat in silence.

From her remote seat Barbara could not hear the rites—the incessant moan from the Negroes drowned out the minister's voice—so she studied the pines beyond, watching the crows dip in and out of the green, until a collective wail rose from the other side of the grave. *The casket must be going down.*

She pivoted on the concrete border and slid onto the brown grass that came right up the stone she'd been hiding behind. She stretched her legs out onto the cold ground, stuck them straight out, no matter the cost to the dress, as a child would do, and leaned back against the stone. When they were gone she would say her good-bye to Amos. Before her lay acres of headstones, whose tops lightly shimmered with noonday sun, and beyond them stretched more pines, as green now as they would be in summer, where the black dots of crows crossed and crossed.

When she peeped around, after what seemed like hours, the crowd was gone. Like a cloudburst followed by a deep, fresh sky the grave site had cleared; only a cluster of blacks remained on the other side of the hole, where they had been all along. She stepped across the border and walked toward the grave, leaning over to look at markers on the way as if she were casually touring the cemetery. The Negroes were moaning and crying, one periodically raising her lament above the others in a high-pitched, tenuous wail like a child or savage who had never learned the proper way to manage grief. *Why won't they go?* She walked closer and closer until she was beneath the canopy and at the very edge of the opening in the ground. The coffin lay deep in the red-clay hole, its bright metal surface an anomaly in the fundamental darkness of the grave. *I will not cry. I will make no sound.* She clenched her lower lip between her teeth and stood in silence.

"Let it out, girl," a voice came from across the grave. "If you feel it, let it out." She looked up. The Negro woman who had been wailing was alone now and looking directly at her. She wore a black dress, slick with wear, and black hat with veil; a red monogrammed initial blazed like a patch of blood on one collar. "You ain't nothing but a nigger too—if it's real, let it out."

Barbara stared through her veil at the tall, lean woman, whose veiled face was puffy, shapeless with sorrow, her eyes so far back in her swollen lids that they were mere points of light. Then her chest heaved and, lifting her face and clenching her fists into tight knots, she broke into her lament again.

Barbara recoiled and ran from the grave, stumbling and clutching until she had reached the safety of the headstone where she had hidden earlier. Even above her gasping she could hear the wail, a piercing sorrow that echoed through the cemetery. She kneeled, her eyes fixed on a clump of almost colorless plastic flowers wedged between the headstone and concrete border. Her eyes blurred with tears, and there beside an anonymous headstone, there in that cemetery shared only by the Negro woman, her grief rose and she sobbed uncontrollably while she heard above her own anguish her dark other self wailing beside the open grave.

ELEANOR'S
CALLER

W H E N she first saw the old man lingering at her gate, Eleanor thought no more about him than she would about *any* reprobate who might have passed her house and paused to rest or loiter. People were always walking over on her side of the street when they might just as well use the other side, where houses were not nearly so old and grand as hers and where whatever flowers grew within reach of the walk would not have been missed by the owners even if someone were desperate enough to want them. But, then, she supposed, that was the problem, wasn't it? Her house *was* the oldest and grandest and her flowers *were* within reach and were lovely and redolent and would be missed, and that explained why every form of rabble the town had to offer slouched past her place, often as not pausing to admire what still was one of the finest houses in East Texas and a yard that had won the Gardening Club monthly award so many times that her heart didn't leap any more when the ladies called with their nice white sign.

And, oh, what a house it was, what a yard, front and back— kept by a bevy of blacks for so many years that she could scarcely recall anyone touching anything inside or outside the house who was not at least remotely related to her family's original stable of slaves. Even now she could hear at her back Isabelle bumbling around in the kitchen preparing lunch and snacks for the ladies who would be visiting later. Somewhere on the lawn or in one of the rose gardens or, more likely, sitting on his lazy rear behind one of the outbuildings languished Uncle Jim-Jim; at noon he would rouse himself from whatever stupor he was in and rattle the back screen, expecting to be fed as if he had labored since first light for her. A cursory inspection would yield little evidence that he had stirred the soil in any of the flower beds or cut a single weed. She wasn't sure whether he was lazy because he was a Negro or because he was a man. Being both was an insufferable affliction.

One of Isabelle's daughters came in twice a week to vacuum, dust, and iron, duties that the older Negro declared her arthritis would not permit her to do without unbearable pain, using her moans and sighs and grunts as evidence that only God should be permitted to lay such burdens on a human being. When things broke down, as it seemed they did with greater and greater frequency these days, Uncle Jim-Jim called in whatever kind of repairman he needed, always someone kin to him—therein lay the sure road to reliability, he said—and always someone who repaired pipe or roof or light switch just well enough to allow him to get out of sight before it broke again. Still, it was infinitely better than dealing with white repairmen from town, who charged enormous fees and fixed things, she knew for a fact from the testimony of victims, no better than her blacks. She preferred to keep things the way she had always known them.

In fact, were it not forbidden by law and well out of social favor, she would have built cabins and kept the Negroes on the place, working them for nothing as her forebears of long ago had done. She acknowledged to herself, when fleeting guilt or at least uncertainty tempered such a notion, that the Negroes had been much better off—physically, socially, and probably financially—when they belonged legally to the Hillman family. Through her family's unflagging benevolence, they were allowed to stay on the land after the War, serving however they could and receiving whatever compensation Nelson Hillman judged appropriate; the descendants of both blacks and whites were still together, though the blacks lived off in their own houses across town and walked or drove to work like anyone else.

They were bitterly poor, Isabelle and Uncle Jim-Jim and all the others who served her, and would remain so until she expired, at which time the whole of the family fortune would pass to them— a fact that she kept carefully hidden in a handwritten will in a safety-deposit box at the bank. The Negroes did not know; not even her attorneys knew that secret. Not one extra penny until then. If they stuck with her, if they served her as they should, they would be richly rewarded. She knew how to rule and how to determine worth in people—by their loyalty, fealty. Laziness was no matter. She expected it of them. She wanted them there, wanted to be served as was declared by her birthright, and she would pay them as little as she could, making certain that those who stayed with her stayed not because of money but because she was who she was.

Built by her great-grandfather before the Civil War, the house sat on a hill near the center of town, and people from God knew where drove by, all hours, just to look at it. It was listed in all sorts of indexes and had a historical marker out front proclaiming its early erection and rich history. Her family had always been wealthy, so nothing was spared in making Hillman House, as it was called, a majestic monument to the family name. Towering three stories, the enormous white house, as richly ornate inside as out, occupied the middle of its own block, dominating the horizon, rising even above the level of the roof of the courthouse, eight blocks or so to the north. One of Eleanor's earliest and fondest memories was clinging to her father's neck as he held her at an upstairs window and pointed down at the town and fields and river bottoms trailing out from it, detailing for her the extent to which the Hillman empire once stretched. "We are above it all," she recalled his saying, "way above the rest of the world, independent of it."

And that philosophy—though she was the last of the line of Hillmans and the old empire was now nothing but a few million dollars dryly drawing interest and a city block of lawn and flowers with a huge white house perched in the middle of it—was what she had lived by. She could not have married if she had wanted, because that would have meant having to give up the Hillman name to some man who could not possibly have been worth the loss. So she remained simply Eleanor Hillman, matriarch and symbol, wealthy and powerful, known and respected. And though she could have reclaimed the sold acres any time she wanted, the money being hers to use any way she wished, she clung as well to another bit of philosophy her father passed on, that one should own only what physical property could be directly possessed, touched, and appreciated. The house and block of lawn and flowers were all the real property she needed. She had ruled properly and performed her nature well. Her father would have been proud.

But the neighborhood was, alas, crumbling, and rabble were moving into houses down the street, especially toward the south, where the fairgrounds were. There was a time when nice houses and fine families lined her street, when the sight of trashy people near the front gate would have been quite extraordinary. Now she was almost amazed when she looked out and did not see some undesirable loitering at the street. Sometimes it bothered her; at other times it troubled her not at all. If things got too bad, she would just buy that side of town, or at least the street, have cotton fields prepared and planted and nice little cottages built, and move her Negroes in. She would tolerate no trash on their lawns, no slatternly kin lying about, no high grass or weedy flowerbeds. One day she'd talk to the lawyers about it.

She was not surprised, then, when she peeped out that morning to see whether the sun would be full or suppressed by clouds and saw slumped against the right-hand column of her iron gate an old derelict who, from what she could tell from her limited perspective, was Caucasian, somewhere in his seventies or eighties, and dreadfully poor. Probably drunk, she surmised when her eyes discovered the bottle neck sticking out of a brown paper bag in his coat pocket.

"I guess I ought to call the Law," she said to herself as she moved to the parlor to get a slightly different angle on him. "No telling what he's been up to." Elderly now—and she would admit to anyone a certain pride at having reached seventy in sound physical and financial condition—she could not be too careful with all the riffraff about. Living alone was her lot by choice, but there were times when she knew that she was vulnerable. Of course, the police would be at her door in five minutes any hour of the day if she called, one advantage of being wealthy and socially respectable, so she saw no need to bother with anyone else in the house, except her day Negroes, to help look after her. "To help look after you" was the way people put it, when what it really amounted to was someone in the house to look after *yourself*, to be certain they didn't steal you blind or set the kitchen on fire or fake your will and poison you and take everything for themselves.

No thank you, she'd look after her own affairs the way she always had and always would, and when it got to the point where she couldn't perform physically or mentally, she kept a friend in her upper dresser drawer that would take care of her problems with one pull of the trigger, which she did not doubt for a second that she would have the resolve to manage when the time came. She'd already called on him twice during her life since her father had used him to solve his last problems, her mother having succumbed years before to a bout of pneumonia. Both times he served quite well, once putting to flight a burglar who had pried open a window and entered her living room, in the process making so much noise that she had armed herself and slipped downstairs and stood waiting for him with the gun leveled at his face by the time he righted himself from a woefully inept entry. When he was on his feet and moving across the living room toward the hallway, his head weaving from side to side like an enchanted snake as he took in what must have been to him a breathtaking panorama of Victorian furniture and original oils and priceless glassware, she flipped on the light and his eyes stopped on the Colt revolver, whose muzzle would shrivel any man in his tracks. His exit was, if not more gracefully, certainly more *quickly* executed.

Another time one of Uncle Jim-Jim's yard boys had made the mistake of bringing two of his thuggy friends by after dark to rummage through one of the outbuildings for God knew what, only to look up from an open trunk, full of nothing but family things, into her flashlight beam eclipsed by that big black barrel. Their retreat was at best an undignified, tail-tucked scramble for the dark of the shrubs on the back side of the garden. She kissed the cold steel of the Colt, more predictable and dependable than any man, and carried it upstairs and to bed with her, where it stayed for weeks afterward, shoved under her pillow, a vague hardness through the soft that reminded her of her father and her own dear, deep strength.

Eleanor Hillman could take care of herself, no matter how gentle her nature and how generous her charity. It had been the lot of the Hillmans to have few children to live to adulthood and her father's particular fate to have only one child, so she had had to be both son and daughter to him. He had taught her strength and courage, common sense and independence, stressing time after time that the day would come when she would be the only Hillman carrying the name in those parts. She intended, as long as she lived, to carry it well.

"You are better than a boy," he told her once as they leaned out an upstairs window looking over the town. His cold, hard eyes bored into her. "You have an inner strength that will allow you to rise above the frivolous and glandular." He pulled her close to him. "I am much better satisfied with you than I could be with a boy. You will carry the name well."

As far as she was concerned, she was an institution in the town, every bit as influential and politically powerful—and without a doubt as wealthy—as all the churches and the two banks put together. Without her money there might be only one bank and it terribly small. Of course, she did what she thought appropriate for the churches and banks. She did not boast about it, because boasting was common, something people who had nothing, or thought they did not deserve what they did have, did.

So there he was, some slovenly old creeper slouched at her gate all morning with the clock pushing one, when ladies from one of the civic clubs were due, ostensibly for a social call. Eleanor

had long ago learned that social calls invariably turned to a re-
quest for charity of some sort, no matter who the callers or their
affiliations. She also learned that she must always manage some
donation, however insignificant, for in that direction lay further loyalty and deference—a penny today to someone asking
for it might mean a dollar's worth of help when she needed it.
No matter what the nature of her need, she had cultivated
enough goodwill and, yes, obligations, from the townspeople
that all she had to do was let it be known and they would jump
to her aid.

Isabelle called to her from the kitchen about something that
she was sure was inconsequential, but she went anyway, peeping
one more time to see whether the old man had moved. He had
not. His body was so nearly prostrate that it was obvious he intended to spend the day there. She'd just call the Law.

When Eleanor returned from the kitchen, though, there was
no sign of him. She even tiptoed out onto the porch and craned
her neck both directions, but he was nowhere along the street.
Just as she let the screen door to behind her, the first of the ladies
arrived and the old man slid into the back of her mind like a
mildly troubling dream.

"You're who?" It was late now and evening settled across the sky
like fine smoke. The old creeper stood squared away before her
door, his hat still jammed down onto his oblong head, which
seemed balanced like an egg on the ropy neck that rose out of his
soiled collar. His coat—a coat in weather hot enough to melt
cheese!—was an old woolen pea coat, once black but now road-
stained until it looked liked something a group of kids might
have tried to age for a school drama. The pants that fell out of it,
smudged and tattered at the cuffs, were misshapen and hung
loosely about what must surely have been legs with only a veneer
of flesh about the bones. The squalid shirt was essentially colorless, with thin dark stripes running vertically; some splatterings
of what looked like coffee stains covered the front, though, God
forbid, they might have been made by anything from chocolate
to feces.

His long-unshaved face could have belonged to a man sixty years old or a hundred—how could you tell about a man who had lived the way he apparently had? She'd seen urchins in the street in poorer areas of town who, though they had the smooth, lean bodies of boys, looked at her with faces so aged by hunger and weather and smoke-filled billiard rooms, fists and knives, that judged by their faces alone they might well have been thought middle-aged men battered almost into submission by the inimical forces that hounded their lives.

"William Hathorne. Bill. Billy Hathorne." He tilted his horse face and squinted in at her. One eye seemed clouded, fogged, dead to light, but she couldn't be sure looking through the mesh of the screen door. He smiled with tight lips when he said his name. Was it supposed to mean something to her? It didn't, though she had sensed somehow as he moved up her walk and mounted the steps—she had watched him drift up the street and right through her gate as if he had gone off somewhere to make up his mind to approach the house—that she had seen him somewhere before, somewhere a long way off in her memory, like someone or something she might have recalled from a book. And perhaps that's where she did remember him from. He certainly looked like something from a piece of fiction, a character created to turn up on a gentlewoman's doorstep to announce that he was her lover from long ago lost in a storm at sea who'd finally found his way back home. And of course against all good sense she would take him in, would have to, and nurse him back to health, only to have him turn out worse than he was before she lost him, a drunkard and villain, abusive of language and cruel to animals and children and women. And after a few months of hell with him she would decide that life was no longer worth living and slip up to her room and remove her revolver from its nest of scented scarves and, after caressing its hard, smooth lines and cocking the hammer, end her misery with one merciful pull of the trigger. Or maybe she'd just kill *him*. Either way.

"Am I supposed to know you, Mr. Hathorne?" She aimed her eyes like ice picks into the lean face that stared through the screen.

"Well, Elner, I was hoping so." He smiled again, though it was quick, like a trap opening and snapping to.

The fact that he knew her name meant nothing. Everyone in town knew it. And though she was sure that he did not live there, he could have picked it up anywhere. "You know my name, I see. Where would I know you from?" She kept her chin thrust out firmly.

"Can I come in?" he asked, reaching out a pale clawlike hand and gripping the screen door handle. With his other hand he scooped off the dark brown hat, squashed and flexed back out so many times that it was a hat in basic function only, that had covered the thin white hair plastered against his skull.

She hooked her hand across the spring that held the door closed and slipped the latch through its eye-screw with the other. "Certainly not, sir. I do not know you." In the back of her mind she could see the Colt nestled in its drawer. She wished it were lying on the table beside her.

"Aw, hell, Elner, you know me." When he smiled this time, it was wider and longer, and she could see that his teeth didn't look as bad as she had thought they would. A little stained, but, the best she could tell, real and fairly straight and all there in front, where they counted. He looked down at his shoes self-consciously and brushed the tops off on his pants legs, as if that would do any good. They looked like shoes that Uncle Jim-Jim might throw away.

"Would you like me to call the Law, or will you leave now?" Hand still hooked on the spring, she was leaning slightly away from the door, putting her weight against him, should he decide to yank and pull the latch loose.

"Billy. Billy Hathorne. Last time I was on this porch—" He grinned again, even wider than before, and dropped his hand back to his side. "Last time I was on this porch you was setting over there in a white chair dressed in a purty yeller dress with white trim, a yeller ribbon in your hair, and real shiny black shoes, like they was polished stones, shiny as your eyes."

The character was stirring in her mind again, the lean old man slouching up her walk, back from the sea and dark, ready to reassume his place in her life. There seemed to be a glow behind him, way behind him, like the sky lit by a terrible fire or a rising blood moon . . . Oh sweet Jesus, God above. She could see the glow at the end of the street as surely as she had that night when he stood on the porch, his long, muscled arm hooked around one of the enormous white columns, and asked her to go with him to the fair. Billy. Billy Hathorne.

"You know now, don't you?" He had not reached out again to the handle. "You remember."

Her father had prepared her for the boys who would come calling. She had heard so many times the hot-bloods panting at the steps, the sharp clatter of their hooves on the porch boards, the clash of horns—and she repulsed them, not rudely, but resolutely, one by one, with an offer of cold lemonade and polite, untouching conversation, turning it always to religion or history or art, but certainly away from the affairs of the flesh. She cared nothing for their leering eyes and lean bodies, their libidinous minds. Her father had instructed her. He knew.

"Would you like to go to the fair?" he asked her, the lean boy who had called. He was from one of her classes at school, but she knew no more about the boys who surrounded her than she knew about the financial markets that her father talked about—and she could not have cared less about either. Her estimation of him, if she had to have one, was that he was awkward and inarticulate and had no earthly notion how to choose or apply cologne, his dousing having forced her to flail her fan vigorously to make the air fit to breathe.

"The fair?" She glanced off down the street toward the glow that suffused the evening sky. Fair. Fair, indeed. It was to her, as her father had taught her and her mother had confirmed, a *carnival*, a place of the flesh, where wild animals and human freaks were displayed for the gawking peasant class and swarthy fellows bellowed out enticements to lure the gullible to their booths, where, she understood, garish dolls and knickknacks could be had for knocking over stacked concrete milk jugs or popping small balloons. And then later, under the glaring lights of an arena, sometimes inside a tent, sometimes out in the open air, foolish men and women on wires high above the upturned faces swung and balanced and defied gravity until the sweaty masses battered their hands in applause.

All her childhood long she got no closer to the fair than her upstairs window, where she could look down toward the glare and the noise of people and music, the top fourth of the Ferris wheel clearly visible in a blazing arc that rose out of the top of one tree and fell into the dark top of another. There were nights when the delicate tinkling of the rides and the shadows of tree limbs on the ceiling and walls lulled her to an uneven sleep in which demons she had never known—buttery fat or thin as snakes or legless— rollicked grotesquely arm in arm with Negroes and white-trash boys. Some nights the roar of the crowd woke her and she sat up, shivering, hands clasped, wondering if the Judgment had come.

Every year it returned, early in September, as regular as Halloween or Christmas. One day the gay posters would appear, tacked here and there to poles and fences, taped to windows in storefronts, great rectangles of yellow and red and black scattered with pictures of animals such as she had never seen and freaks and fat women and men whose limbs were stretched like rubber bands. At the top, above the bold declaration of Fair Week, teetered a stone-faced man on a shining wire. A child sat on his shoulders, a little girl whose expression remained the same, year after year, as the posters appeared, faded, and were taken down by people or the wind. A week or so after the posters splashed across town, Eleanor would hear the heavy trucks grinding by out front, then hammering and yelling for two days, a burst or two of music, and the torrent of people would begin in the street. For a week the night sky would be filled with light and noise.

One morning when she was in junior high she went down to breakfast in the middle of Fair Week and overheard her father and mother discussing the noise of the night before, a particularly loud night that had kept her awake until the early hours. "What I ought to do," he said, bringing his fist down on the table, "is buy that whole Goddamn end of town and have that fairground plowed up and planted in cotton. It might not make money for us, but I never saw a cotton field in my life that made noise or one that people wanted to go and throw money away in." He quieted when he saw Eleanor in the doorway but went on speaking. "I could put a stop to that damned foolishness."

But the week was over quickly and he forgot about the fair, and so it continued, year after year. She had never asked to go, though many children had invited her, male and female. Her father told her that it was not an appropriate place for young ladies of culture, her mother nodded in agreement, and it was settled—she never went. Her social life was limited, as was befitting one of her station in life, to church functions and certain events involving the wealthy of the county. Her father drove her to school, arriving precisely at eight o'clock and picking her up promptly at the last bell. Though he never said so, she was certain that he felt the other children unworthy of her company—he kept them at a comfortable distance. Her parties, the few that there were, were largely adult affairs attended by her father's friends and associates, with a couple of children of wealthier families in town invited to make Eleanor happy. "Being around grown-ups will mature you properly," he once told her. Her mother nodded.

She accepted her loneliness as one of the prices to be paid by the wealthy and powerful, a social sacrifice, so she pleasantly repulsed any efforts by other children to entice her out among them. Her parents had elected to self-teach her the last two years of high school, bringing in tutors when subjects required it, and they gave her a choice of whether or not to go off to college, making it quite clear that they would prefer that she not leave. She chose to stay home, where a copious library and her father's bountiful mind provided her with all she needed to know.

After reaching adulthood, she seldom left the house, preferring the company of her family or books or no company at all. When she did venture out, the trips were brief, quiet affairs: She slid into the back seat of their luxury sedan, through whose tinted windows she could see the shadowy outer world but no one could see her, and her father or Uncle Jim-Jim or whoever happened to be handy whisked her away and back. She saw little beyond the confines of their yard that made her wish to live her life any differently. There had been times when she felt a mild compulsion to be among other people, but when she was there she felt dreadfully uncomfortable and longed to be back home. When later in life a desire to venture out possessed her, she merely remembered who she was and returned to her room and stared at the portrait of her stone-faced father until the feeling was suppressed. Some years after her father's death, the old stirrings for a social life finally disappeared entirely, and she settled into a quiet, firm reign over all that was hers.

She had leveled her eyes at the boy Billy Hathorne that evening and said simply, "No, I would not care to go to the carnival." And she emphasized the word so that it tasted vile on her tongue.

He stood clinging to the column like a half-tame monkey, grinning, staring off toward the bright sky. A thin moon that looked like a set of bull horns seemed to be balanced by a tip on the top of his head. "Well . . . ," he began, then trailed to nothing.

"What is that you are wearing?" she asked.

He arched his long neck and look at his shirt front and pants.

"No, no, that odor you are reeking of. What is that?"

"Oh," he answered shyly, "that's some of my daddy's stuff that I got out of the bathroom. It's 'sposed to make me smell like a man. You like it?"

"It smells like—" Then she remembered who she was. "It is certainly an unusual smell. Do you think you put enough on?"

"I don't know. I ain't never wore any before. I put it on for you."

She forced a smile. "How very kind."

"They's a man eight feet tall down there." He pointed toward the glow. "And a fat woman with jaws like a hog that weighs nearly four hundred pounds and can play 'Dixie' with her armpit. Think you'd like to go, maybe?"

"I certainly would not," she answered coolly. "If I want to hear 'Dixie,' my father will sing it for me."

"But what about the tall man and the fat lady? You can't find them just everwhere, and there's a two-headed calf besides."

She lifted her nose and aimed it at him. "My father is tall enough, well over six feet. Fat people are common—there's nothing attractive about being fat. And a two-headed calf would just be repulsive." She screwed her face up and settled deeper into the porch chair. "If you want to be with me," she told him decisively, "it'll have to be here at my home."

He shook his head and looked off down the street toward the sound of music from the carnival. "I guess I'll go on then, to the fair." He started down the steps. He turned and looked up at her. "You don't never go nowhere, do you?"

"I don't need to. I have all that I want right here." She swept her arms from left to right and circled her head. "I can't see that I need much more." He left at that, passed through the gate and, without waving good-bye, joined the people who were flowing in that direction, like filth washing down the gutter toward some loathsome gathering place where the surface glare was, she knew, underpinned by the dark magnetism of Satan himself.

"Well, the fair's there and I'm going and I'd like you to go with me," the old man said. "Look and listen, Elner—the music's fine, ain't it? And there's a glowing there, a brightness. Look over there, Elner." He pointed to the bright arc against the sky. "There's a shining."

She folded her arms for all reply.

"Elner, this is your last chance. I'm all you got, all you ever gon' have. I've had more women than you could count rosebuds in your flower beds, and you ain't never had a man."

"You don't know what or whom I've had, Billy Hathorne, and it's no business of yours one way or the other."

"Elner, you ain't had any life but what they gave you in this house. You have violated nature, woman—you ain't had a man and you ain't had a child. I wouldn't doubt that you ain't ever been kissed on the mouth by a man."

She stared hard at him. "None of any of my business is any of yours, Mr. Hathorne. If you want to go to the fair, as you call it, then go along. Just get off my porch and begone—somewhere." She stood back from the screen and threw out her arms and hands as if she were trying to drive away some strange animal from her door.

"They still got a fat woman and a rubber man and a alligator boy, Elner, still got all them animals, and the big-top ain't changed one whit. Oh, the people's all changed out, a'course—all of them that was alive back then is probably dead, but fat women always keep coming, and there's always animals, and as long as there's somebody to pay to see it, there'll be people walking across wires. It's all new, Elner, but it's the same. Come on, girl, let's go." He grasped the handle of the screen door and pulled.

"Mr. Hathorne, I'll ask you this once more to get on away from here. If you won't go, I'll have to call the police."

He smiled and nodded, adjusting the hat on his head, then descended the steps a second time, his slight figure shambling out to blend with the shadows on the walk, reappearing briefly in the faint glow of a streetlight. She stood on the porch watching as he tipped his hat with a flourish and disappeared into the night toward the mounting music and blazing sky.

When he had disappeared, she slipped out onto the porch and looked all about the lawn and up and down the street. He was gone, vanished into the night as surely as if he had never been there, and she shook her head lightly to clear it. She mounted the steps and reached out to the nearest column, steadying her trembling body. The cool, hard surface reassured her and after one more careful sweep of the yard she went inside.

Returning to her room, she stood at the window staring down the street in the direction he had gone, toward the laughter and applause and music, toward the bright arc of sky she had so many times as a girl and young woman leaned at the window and heard and seen. He was right, right about at least that: nothing had changed much. It was the same music, the same laughter and shouting and applause, the same people moving toward the glow and, she supposed, drifting back past in the dark toward their dreary homes. Strangely, after a few minutes she felt tears coming into her eyes, so she removed the pistol from its drawer, placed it beneath her pillow, and lay down for sleep, fingers pressed to her ears to shut out the music and noise of the distant crowd. She could feel the gun through the pillow, a hard lump against the back of her head, and in the willowy shadows on the wall the face of her father stared down.

What the hell right did Billy Hathorne have talking to her that way? She could have him arrested and put in jail with just a phone call, no questions asked, and they would keep him as long as she wanted them to. When you had money you could get things done to your satisfaction.

Billy Hathorne didn't know *anything* about her. Where had he been all these years? Probably off in the penitentiary at Huntsville, judging by his appearance. He didn't know who she'd kissed and who she hadn't or whether she had had men or not, and for all he knew she could have been living in Europe for decades and just returned. The audacity! But, then, she couldn't be troubled too much by the words of a man who, at his age, still went to the carnival, like a silly child. Just a filthy, silly old manchild.

Sometime later she awoke from a troubled sleep. It might have been a few minutes or hours, but the music still rose from beyond the trees and the shadows of limbs wove dark patterns on the ceiling and walls. She felt fleshless, total spirit, balanced on her father's shoulders high over a dark pit at whose bottom throngs of strange people roared and applauded, her only tie to reality the lump that pressed up through her pillow and forced itself against the back of her brain. The glow from the window grew brighter and brighter, the music louder, until she was sitting straight up in bed trembling like a child.

And then she was running, barefooted, half stumbling, her nightgown trailing out behind as she descended the stairs and flung open the front door to a rush of night air. "Mr. Hathorne!" she called to the dark lawn. "Billy! Billy." The street opened before her, a few astonished people returning from the fair stepping back to let the wild-eyed woman in white pass, turning and watching as she ran toward the music and the glow. Before her, against the sky, higher than she could ever have imagined, rose the lights of the carnival, a colossal dome under which she was drawn faster and faster until she felt shavings under her feet and saw on all sides the spinning faces of the crowd. Beyond the edge of the dome night began again, ringed with sharp-pointed stars and a horned moon.

THE
HUNT

An old man now, wise and wealthy, with over a dozen grandchildren and three great-grandchildren, whose squeals and laughter presently drifted up the stairs of the elegant house to his study, he sat staring through the window that he left open, winter and summer, at the land that rolled off into the distance; over it slid isolated July clouds that traversed the West Texas sky but rarely did more than pass like the shadow of a man's hand over the stretches of small oaks, mesquite clumps, and scrubby pastures, with here and there a jackpump pecking away. It was yet a wild, unsavory land where few made more than a subsistence living—only the lucky and daring and rapacious, willing to reach not simply out, but down deep beneath the harsh landscape into the dark, rich bowels of the earth, as he had.

Even while he sat there gazing, with the trilling children darting about over the lawn, he knew that other eyes were watching from beside and behind, cold and glassy and unblinking, and that reflected in each of them was the Sharps carbine on the wall above his desk, an enormous mushroomed bullet dangling by a thin gold wire looped on the end of the barrel.

* * *

The man rode strange in the saddle. The boy first saw him break the skyline to the southeast just as he looked from behind a small scrub oak on his stalk down the river. He had come up from the water's edge an hour before, after his ration of bread and pork strips, the gritty taste of the river still on his tongue. From the breeze off the water he knew the wind was still from the south and that he had to range farther and farther away from his upriver camp, moving always into the wind and toward whatever game might be drifting down for a drink or forage in the woods along the stream. His chances would doubtless be better just before nightfall, but he had seen no game all day, except for a couple of squirrels very early, and an urgency drove him. By now his father would have had a deer cut up and wrapped in its skin, stowed behind him on the mule, and be on his way home.

"But I am not him," he said out loud as he eased from tree to tree down the river, "and he never trained me for this." The carbine felt awkward and ponderous in his arms as he moved. He stopped and listened for leaves rustling, studying the curve of the hammer as it rose out over the receiver of the Sharps. He had never even shot it, didn't know how much noise it would make— it might even break his shoulder when he pulled the trigger. But fire he would, he knew, when the time came, when the blade of the sight stopped on the neck or shoulder of a deer. And he knew further that when he pulled the trigger he would not miss. *I have come too far, and too many people are depending on me.*

After his brief meal, which would not satisfy him until the fall of night when he would have to give up the hunt and return to his camp, trusting to better luck in the morning, he elected to work the edge of the woods away from the river. There he might spot deer feeding off the scant grass of the slopes and get a shot, perhaps a longer one than he might wish, but a shot. As he held the carbine before him, he wished it were one of the old buffalo Sharps he'd heard about, which a man could prop on a stick and kill a skinny Comanche with at three hundred yards, a full-grown buffalo bull at half a mile. He knew that a successful shot with the carbine would be at less than a hundred yards.

But at least I won't be dodging arrows or bouncing along on a horse trying to aim behind the ear of a running buffalo.

The rider was mounted on either a small horse or a mule—he couldn't tell at such a distance—and he was headed almost directly downwind toward the boy. He stepped back behind the oak and dropped to his knees to study this intrusion on his hunt. Any deer that might have been feeding along the edge of the trees would long ago have been spooked, probably through the woods and across the river, and he doubted that they would come out again until morning. Then again, he *could* flush something toward the boy, if he rode down into the trees.

So the young hunter watched as the figure, who kept to the high ground along the valley rim, grew against the sky. He was probably nearly a half mile away when he pulled his horse up and shaded his eyes into the afternoon sun. There was still nothing distinctive about him, except that he wore a hat and rode a small animal and across his legs or right behind him he balanced a long rifle.

The hunt forgotten now, though he intended to be ready if game flushed toward him, the boy studied the rider, who, after apparently satisfying himself that he had found a good place to hunt or camp or at least water himself and his horse, turned down the slope to the woods and the river. He rode slowly, hunched over in the saddle as if scanning the ground for signs of game or the tracks of other horsemen. He was either a heavy man, the boy decided, or he was wearing a bulky robe of some sort—he was almost as large as the animal he urged along.

When the man disappeared into the woods, the boy slipped back down to the water's edge to see whether he might not be able to get a better view of him as he came to the river to drink— if that's what he intended to do. The river curved slightly just downstream, making a shallow bend, where anyone dropping down to the water would be in clear view against the white rocks. Squatting behind a clutter of flotsam left from the last high water, he cradled the carbine in his arms, eyes fixed downriver, and settled down to wait.

* * *

If the rider ever approached the water, the boy did not see him, but just as evening was settling on the river and the southern breeze was turning sharper, he smelled woodsmoke and a few minutes later saw wisps of it eddying up the bank. At least he knew now that the stranger had set up camp and would probably not be moving on until morning; he knew as well that his chances of getting a deer were remote with someone upwind of him.

Satisfied that even if the rider came to the river now it would be too dark to tell anything about him, the boy rose and walked out to the edge of the woods, where returning to his camp would be easier than trying to weave through the trees in the dark. He turned several times to see whether there was any sign of the stranger behind him, but there was only the darkening tree line along the river and above it the beginning stars.

As he stared into his meager fire—he dared not build a large one with someone else on the river, especially since he knew nothing of the nature of the interloper—he rolled over and over in his hands the five large cartridges that fit the Sharps. He had watched his father melt the lump of lead from which the family had made bullets for years, pour the silvery stream into a dark steel mold, and dump out one fifty-caliber slug after another until the five lay cooling in a tray of sand on his mother's kitchen table. "I am loading up five of these for you, Cleet," he said as he stood five brass cases in a line, "and that ought to do you. If you can't get a deer with five, you can't with ten, so five it is. Besides, if I loaded up ten, you might decide to shoot ten, and we ain't got the caps to spare. And I'm loading'm light to save powder, so you got to get close." He watched intently as his father pressed a primer into each case, seating it with a wooden peg, then poured a measure of powder in each, followed by the slugs, wedged in by hand.

He would not be sitting by the fire nearly twenty miles from home, holding a Sharps carbine in his arms and dreaming of killing a deer at sunup, if his father had not been housebound with a festering leg, which even yet might have to be removed. Ripped open by the deflected blade of an axe, the leg swelled and reddened until the doctor from Cisco was summoned, a stern-faced man who shook his head when the blanket was pulled back and the feed-sack wrapping removed. He did what he could but left with both the reassurance that the father would probably live and the admonition that he might never have to buy boots in pairs again.

With winter coming on and the fields of their small farm laid by until spring, it was the boy's charge to ride out and secure winter meat for the family, there being no cow on the place to spare, no money to buy one for slaughter, and not enough chickens for eating to get them past Thanksgiving. The one pig they had been raising had wandered off or been stolen, and though they had been fortunate enough to enjoy a fair harvest of corn and the summer garden had produced a surplus, without an abundance of salted and dried meat a family could hardly be said to be doing much more than surviving.

"By spring," his father confided in him one night, "I'll be able to get meat again or I'll never be able to get meat again. Your grandfather came back from the War, as you well know, with both legs busted up real bad and he never did come to use them again."

The boy nodded, recalling the story he'd heard over and over how the family came in from a trip to Abilene, found the old man gone from the house, and after following a line of furrows where he had dragged himself to the barn discovered him in a stall with the Sharps beside him, half of his face splattered against a wall.

"You got to be my legs, Cleet, my legs and eyes and arms, something that my daddy, I guess, figured I could be for him. Otherwise he would not have blowed his head off."

It was then that his father explained that the family had to have meat and that the boy must ride out and hunt it down. He would take a mule and the Sharps, ride to the woods along the Colorado, where deer were abundant, and camp until he killed a large deer or two small ones, enough meat, if they rationed properly, to stock them until his father was able to hunt or until he sent the boy out again.

When he lifted the lump of lead from its bag for melting and molding, he handed it to the boy. "Cup it in your hand, son, and you'll feel the life of the family there. This chunk of lead has come down to us from long before the War. The bullets in it have killed deer and wild hogs and at least one bear, and I can't remember more than a couple of times that lead has left it and not come back home to it." He fell silent for a few seconds upon saying that—the boy knew why.

Then his father continued. "When you kill a deer, the first thing you do is dig out the bullet and stick it in your pocket; then bleed him and cut him up and smear your face with blood. First you take out the bullet. The brass and the bullet comes back home with you. We ain't got the brass to spare, and the lead— well, that's just family tradition that I wouldn't want broken. It means, of course, that you can't miss," he concluded, patting the boy on the head.

So on the chosen morning the boy rode out to the southwest, mounted on one of the mules, the Sharps shoved down in a canvas scabbard beside his right leg. He carried tied to the worn saddle a small leather bag of pork strips and still-warm bread, and on the other side a quart jug of water, enough to last him until he reached the river. His mother and child-sized grandmother walked along with him until he finally turned and told them that he would be all right. His father had explained well how to find the river, and within three days he would be back, with deer meat. While he was looking back at them, he could see his sister waving at a window and his father propped in the doorway. And then, turning his head away from them and not lifting his hand to wave, the boy kicked the mule into a trot.

"It wasn't half bad," he said proudly, stirring his fire. "I rode like a man. I may be just thirteen, but I rode like a man and I found the river before dark and tomorrow I am going to kill a deer. Today I was just learning how to hunt." He cupped his hand under the blocky receiver of the Sharps and lifted it before his eyes. "Tomorrow I will know what it is like to shoot it."

He fished out the last of his pork strips and a lump of cold bread, ate them, and swallowed deep from the jug, which he had filled twice that day from the river. "I wish it was whiskey," he said to the mule, tied at the edge of the fire glow, "so I would be even more of a man." At that he spread out one blanket to lie on and pulled the other one over him, positioning himself so that during the night he could reach his pile of wood and throw more onto the fire without getting up. Then he tried to sleep.

But sleep would not come. If the man downriver had not been there, or if the boy had not known he was there, perhaps he would have been able to ignore the night sounds from the river and woods—the murmur of the water and the nightbirds, an occasional rustle in the leaves. But he *was* there and the boy knew it. And whether he was a cowboy riding up to Abilene or a hunter or some fugitive from the Law, there was no way of knowing, short of going down to take a look. His father had reassured him that he was likely to encounter no one else on his hunt and that if he did he was to keep his distance and mind his own business. "Ain't nobody would trouble you for that scrawny mule, except maybe a Mexican, and I doubt that anybody wanting the Sharps, Mexican or outlaw or whatever, would be willing to risk the chance of you pointing that cannon barrel at him and pulling the trigger."

The more the boy's imagination worked, the more ominous his wilderness companion became. *If it's a Mexican renegade, he could be slipping up on my camp right now, he could be aiming his gun at me right now or waiting until I'm asleep to push a knife into me.* He pulled the Sharps up under his blanket, jacked it open, and slid in one of the heavy cartridges from his pocket.

But there was little comfort lying there with a loaded gun when his enemy might well be at the edge of his small clearing with a rifle trained on him, quite ready to blow his head off. He twisted and surveyed the low growth and trunks of scrub oaks about him—anyone with any stealth at all could get within handgun range and fire before he could think of pulling up the Sharps.

Even when he slid the carbine out and laid it alongside him, cocked, he felt no more secure. So, knowing nothing else to do, the boy pulled on his boots and, after tying the mule away from the glow of the dying fire and stashing his saddle and water jug behind a tree, uncocked the carbine and headed downstream.

* * *

Aware that even if he were fully familiar with the woods he could not hope to move silently through them in the moonless dark, he kept to the outside edge, where the open grassland to his left sloped up and ridged against the night sky. He could see nothing except the scattered trees immediately before him, so he worked his way upwind, stopping and smelling the air, then moving again. He was grateful that the wind was still from the south. When at last he reached what he judged to be the spot where he had seen the man that afternoon, he turned down to the river, carefully making his way through undergrowth and around tree trunks and the clutter of flood drift until he stood where he could see, profiled by white rocks along the waterline, the long river bank that curved back to his right.

And there, a quarter of a mile downstream and not a dozen steps from the water and the rocks he had watched as the sun set, flickered a campfire, from which the faint smell of woodsmoke drifted to him.

Once again the boy was stalking, this time moving downriver and upwind not toward the uncertainty of ghostly deer, which he had not even had the fortune of seeing, but toward the certainty of the other man's fire, which, fortunately or not, he *had* seen. He was out at the grassy edge of the woods, where he could walk with little noise, and though he could only guess when he had come even with the stranger's camp, he knew that by easing back down to the river he could pinpoint it again with no difficulty.

He did not have to return to the river. As he slipped from behind a small clump of bushes a few yards above where he calculated the camp to be, his eye caught a flash of firelight through the trees. *It is him. I have found him.*

The crawl through night woods toward the little circle of light was more difficult than he had imagined, and even with the wind rising now in the trees overhead and stirring the underbrush, he was afraid that with every move of an arm or leg he would alert the figure whose vague outline he came slowly to make out against the dark woods beyond the fire. He kept the

Sharps thrust out ahead so that should he be set upon he would have only to cock the gun and fire.

After what seemed an eternity to the boy he lay at the north edge of the man's campsite behind an oak trunk thick as a bushel basket, the barrel of the carbine pushed out past the tree and aimed generally at the bulky figure slumped against a tree across from where he lay. He had not looked up at the man in the last few feet of his crawl, fearing that if he looked he would see the eyes of the stranger on him. It was better to worry that the man might have heard and seen him than to be certain that he had and look across the fire into the end of a pistol. If he had to die that very night, he wanted it to be a surprise.

And when he looked, when he finally summoned the nerve to press his face hard against the oak and pivot until an eye could draw the figure in, he could not believe what, through the shimmer of heat from the fire, he was seeing. Not twenty feet from him, with a hat pulled down over his forehead and an animal-skin rug drawn up over his body to the chin, an enormous Indian slept. On a bundle of some sort of skins beside him lay a long rifle, whose barrel, large in bore as a shotgun, pointed out over the boy's head.

He pulled his head behind the oak and dropped his face into the crook of his left elbow. God, what had he gotten himself into? An Indian, a full-grown Indian warrior with a buffalo rifle, slumped against a tree within spitting distance. It couldn't be, it just couldn't be. There weren't any Indians on the Colorado. They had all been defeated and herded off to reservations in Oklahoma years before he was born. People still talked about them, the bloody raids down from the High Plains on nights of the Comanche moon, murder and rape, kidnapping and pillage, leaving nothing but smoldering ruins of cabins and barns and a trail of bloody clothes and tracks that disappeared completely in the sea of grass to the northwest. But all that, now that he was almost a man, was just stale legend and held no reality for him. He had never seen an Indian, not even a tame one, except once near Cisco, when he thought a mounted man being towed by a rope behind a marshal might have been an Indian, but at the distance he saw him could just as well have been a Negro or Mexican or Arab.

He could remember lying on the roof of the barn for long hours when he was younger, staring across the fields, hoping that he might see the dust of a Comanche war party or a lone warrior. He imagined himself a sentinel who would sound the alarm, then clamber down from the roof and snatch the Sharps from its closet corner, the old Colt percussion revolver from beneath the bed, and, alongside his father, engage in fierce battle until all the Indians lay dead before them.

And there were the nights of the full moon when he slipped from his bed and moved through the shadows of the house and barn and sheds, his eyes ever on the bright fields where here and there low trees broke the horizon. Behind any one of them Comanches could be crouched, ready to assault the house if he but relaxed his guard. There were times when, though he may have nodded off a few seconds during his long night of vigil, he did not return to his bed until the eastern sky began to lighten.

But the Indians never came, not a war party, not a single warrior, and as the years wore on his days were filled more and more with plowing and building fences and the thousand other labors that stole a boy's time and so tired him that when he wasn't working he was too weary to dream. As he too quickly became something closer to a man than a boy, the Comanches faded and disappeared from his mind as surely as they had from the Plains.

So his mind raced as he lay deathly quiet behind the oak, his face buried in his arm, the Sharps still pointed toward the sleeping man. He dared not try to back out, now that he knew who—or what—the intruder was. He could only lie in stark and utter fear with his heart pounding against the cold ground, gripped in a stasis that would let him do no more than think and breathe. By whatever stretch of luck he had managed to crawl undetected up to the campsite, he could not bring himself to try to crawl back out to the grassy plain to his left or down to the river, which he could hear swishing and gurgling to his right.

By hiding the carbine in the brush, he might be able to move more silently through the moist leaves down to the water, slide in and cross the river, walk up to his camp and cross back over, and ride away in the dark into the hills, then come back down late in the day, when the man ought to be gone, and retrieve the Sharps. But he would no more leave the carbine, he knew, than he would leave his right leg. The Indian might find it next morning, making him even more dangerous with two rifles, or, worse yet, discover the boy slipping unarmed down to the river and murder him with a knife in the dark. He could unload and pocket the cartridge, rendering the Sharps useless to the Indian, but he would still be losing the carbine, which he could not imagine explaining to his father.

But the matter of the gun paled before a more insistent thought now drumming in his mind: What of the Indian? Armed and mounted, a lone warrior could raid a dozen isolated farmhouses and reduce them and their inhabitants to ashes before word got out that he was rampaging. There was no knowing what mischief the buck had already been up to, where he was coming from or going to, what scalps or booty lay wrapped in the skins beside him. He might have stolen the short, scrawny horse tied at the edge of the camp, might have killed for it, and the gun itself had to have been taken from a white man somewhere, since Indians were forbidden to have them.

The nearest lawman that he knew anything about was in Cisco, and he had no earthly notion where to find a ranger or a soldier, even if by some miracle he could crawl into the open, run to his camp, and ride off in the dark. By the time he managed to urge the mule to Cisco or Abilene or one of the forts to the north, it would be well past daylight, assuming he could find his way back over the trail without even a moon to help him. He thought of tying the mule in the trees and striking out on foot, as he knew any Indian surely would do, making better time than he could on what was probably, in the dark, worse than no mount at all, but the heavy field boots on his feet would wear him down the first mile—and there was the gun to be carried, and water. No, he would have to dog the mule the best he could, if he could get to him.

If he got crossed up in the night, the landmarks his father had so carefully laid out swallowed by the great moonless prairie, he might be two days or longer getting to the authorities. And then there was the trip back south, a good half day's ride on a fast horse. No matter how he looked at it, the Indian would be two days away, in any direction, by the time he brought anyone back. In two days a lot of houses could burn and a lot of people die.

A stick popping in the fire brought him back to the little circle of light before him. Raising his head ever so slowly, he pressed his right cheek against the cold stock of the Sharps and sighted along the barrel until the Indian, less distinct now in the light of the dying fire, came into focus. He appeared not to have moved. The boy studied the dark figure, raising the front sight from the middle of the massive robe, where his chest should be, to the hat, then dropping just below it, holding steady, steady until the sight stopped quivering and the Indian's hawklike nose shaped itself between the hat rim and the edge of the robe. *He is so big. He is one of the biggest men I have ever seen.*

His little world wound tightly about him, the boy lay beneath the simple and distant stars with the night wind playing up steadily from the south, his body pressed to the solid earth, while to his right the river rushed off to places he had never seen and would probably never go and around him hovered dark trees that offered no solace. There was nothing to comfort him, nothing to give answer to his racing mind—there was only the Indian and the night and him. He stared into the dark mass of the robe, dropped the sight of the Sharps until it trembled somewhere in the center, cupped his hand over the hammer to mute its click, and, holding the sight as steady as he could, closed his eyes and fired.

Sprawled behind the drift log with the Sharps pointed in the direction the Indian would come from, the boy tried to calm his pounding heart and recall the shot and his frantic retreat through night woods, past the campsite and tethered mule, to the defensive position he had taken. The flash and incredible roar—the one still dancing behind his eyes as he stared into the dark, the other ringing in his ears—he could compare to nothing in his memory, except perhaps to the day lightning sundered a nearby tree along the creek where he and his family were picnicking, scattering them like frightened hens. But then the flash and sound came unexpectedly, just as he was reaching for a piece of bread, and its coming was unreal, as if in a dream. He had known the gunshot was coming as soon as his finger reached a certain point, and he had waited for it with his breath suspended, his eyes unblinking, his ears fine-tuned to the night sounds about him. And when it came, it was more real than anything he had ever known, the flash and sound and unbelievable jolt of the butt to his shoulder telling him that the gun had indeed fired—and that what he had fired it at was another human being.

Only the stumbling plunge upstream through dark trees and underbrush that tore at his body seemed like a dream. In almost slow motion he rolled back with the recoil and turned, scrambling first on his knees and hands, dragging the Sharps by the barrel, then rising to his feet, still using his free hand to thrust himself forward, and finally balancing on his feet in a frantic run toward the edge of the woods. Once he broke out, he never looked back until he had covered the distance that, to the best of his judgment, separated their camps. Then he stopped and dropped to his belly and scanned the stretch of grass behind him, from the dark trees up to the lighter horizon. Eyes still sweeping the expanse of grass and line of woods, he jacked out the spent case, noting that it was still hot to his hand, and slid in a fresh round. Seeing nothing move, he rose, and, glancing once at the dancing stars overhead, dove into the woods again, pausing at his campsite only long enough to snatch up a blanket. When he heard the ripple of the river immediately before him, he fell into a prone position behind the nearest cover, a washed-up log, and aimed the Sharps downstream.

There was no way of knowing whether his shot had killed the Indian or even if he had hit him, though he could not imagine

missing at that distance. What he did know was that if the Indian were still alive, he would be in pursuit, and the boy intended
to be ready.

The long night was a roiling mix of dream and awareness. On
his belly, his face pressed against the log before him, the Sharps
laid across the log and aimed downstream toward the Indian's
camp, the boy used only his ears to alert him of a threat from
that direction, knowing that in the moonless dark his eyes
would merely make Indians of shadows of trees and bushes. If he
came through the woods, wounded and enraged as he would
have to be, he probably would not move with the usual stealth of
an Indian—and if he came up the river, using the sound of the
water to deaden his movement, the boy would see him as he
came up the slope. The night sky, lighter than the woods along
the river, reflected off the water, leaving a backdrop against
which a man would stand out clearly. It was in that direction
that he kept his eyes.

But the Indian did not come. The long night of staring at the
river and listening to the woods, punctuated by terrifying lapses
into dreams of Comanche moons and marauding Indians with
bloody scalps staining their horses' sides, gave way finally to a
brightening sky and trees and bushes and the steaming water.
Cold and stiff in his blanket, he lay long and watched the river
move past, trying to sort out the night before. When at last he
did turn his face away from the river, his neck ached as if someone had taken it and spun it completely around on his shoulders,
snapping sinews and muscle. He moved it back and forth until
the pain subsided, then lifted to look over the log. Only misty
woods lay before him.

Clutching the Sharps, he slithered down the slope to the river
and splashed his face and arms, noting the deep scratches and
welts where vines and thorns had torn at him the night before. *I
didn't feel nothing.* After rinsing out his mouth and drinking
deeply, he sat up and stared off down the river, but there was no
motion, no sound, and the slight south breeze did not smell of
woodsmoke, so he rose and eased to his campsite. Nothing had

changed. The fire was dead white ashes, his saddle had not been touched, and the mule stood where he had been tied the day before. The boy checked to see that no crumbs of bread remained in his bag before walking up to the edge of the woods and staring into the rising sun downstream.

"I have to go, I have to," he said finally. Off to the north lay home and family and all that brought order to his life, but that world was a day's ride away. "I have to know."

The Indian was slumped against the tree exactly as before, the robe still about him, hat pulled low over his eyes, and the rifle lay unmoved on the bundle of skins near the small mound of gray ashes that had been his fire. Only the little horse stirred, twitching his tail from time to time, and birds broke the morning stillness, flitting about the edge of the clearing. It was almost as if he were seeing the clearing for the first time.

Maybe I dreamed it, all of it. But the memory of the roar and flash and the still-hot shell in his hand drummed louder and louder in his mind as he sprawled behind the same tree that had shielded him the night before, staring across the ashes at the Indian. If the man had not awakened at his approach, had not moved a fraction since the shot, he was not likely ever to awake and move on his own again. He was, the boy realized, simply and profoundly *dead*.

He turned onto his back and stared into the deep blue of the sky. The sun had already chased away the stars, and copper-tinged puffs of clouds trundled across from the south. *What do I do now? What do I do with him?* If he rode to Cisco and brought back the sheriff, someone might stumble across the campsite and claim the Indian before they got back; besides, if the sheriff rode into town with the body in tow, *he* would get the credit for stopping whatever rampage the Indian had been on.

He rolled back onto his stomach and stared across the clearing at the dark form leaning against the tree. "I will," he said, rising to his feet, "take him home and ask my father what to do with him. He will know." With the Sharps trained on the slouched figure, he stepped from behind his tree and one slow step at a time crossed the clearing until he stood directly over the Indian.

He touched the gun barrel to top of the man's hat and tapped. Nothing. No response. He moved the barrel to the Indian's shoulder and nudged, but again there was no reaction. *He is dead. I did it—I killed myself an Indian.* With a whoop he thrust the Sharps into the air and shuffled around the ashes of the fire, dancing and laughing, giddy with the victory that was his.

Only when he was breathless with celebration did he pause and fall to his knees before his enemy and discover that the face beneath the hat was not the fierce and defiant visage of an Indian brave in his prime but that of a man older than his grandmother, wrinkled, collapsed, and toothless. When he pushed the stiff body over, what rolled out of the stinking robe cocoon was a dark, coiled thing of skin and bones smaller than he could believe, smaller than his birdlike grandmother. *Oh, my God, what have I done?*

Holding his breath against the stench of urine and feces and a rush of indefinable odors, the boy rolled the man onto his back and saw the hole, barely stained with blood, just below the breastbone. There had been no hole in the back. The bullet was still in him. It had not gone through.

He sat back and stared at the tiny figure before him. He looked like a baby bird, only bigger and darker and without feathers yet, like something that was supposed to fly but didn't have wings. It was then that the boy glanced at the rifle lying across the bundle of skins. An old flintlock, the gun was absurdly long and ungainly looking, rust encrusted, the stock almost burned away, and where the hammer should have curled up there was a stud where one had been. Probably dragged from the ashes of an old home fire, as a weapon it was no more useful than a stick. He looked back at the man.

The boy sat back on his legs and stared a very long time at the first dead man he'd ever seen, stretched out like cold leather, killed by a bullet *he* had fired. The lean little horse stirred as a gust of wind burst through the trees overhead and he knew suddenly who he was and where and what he had to do. Slipping his knife from its sheath, he placed the tip into the bullet hole and drove the blade in until he felt it strike ribs or backbone or bullet—he wasn't sure. He made a slit, working the knife around until he had an opening large enough to accommodate his hand, and plunged his fingers through the gray skin into the Indian's abdomen. Holding his breath, he felt around in the cold, slippery dark until his fingers closed on the bullet, flattened against the backbone. When he withdrew his hand, black with blood, his mind flashed to the time he had watched his father take a difficult calf. Beyond that, he tried not to think at all.

Then the Indian was at the bottom of the river, wrapped in the old robe with rifle and skins and three large stones, rolled into the deepest water the boy could find, his horse driven off beyond the near hills. With a few scoops of leaves scattered over the campsite, it looked like the rest of the woods. He walked to the river bank and scrubbed away at his hand with mud and sand until the blood was gone and his hand shone white in the sun.

He rode home without a deer that afternoon. The hunting was poor, he would tell them, and he had run out of food and had to come home. He would have to try again in a few days. The empty shell in his pocket he could explain away to his father as a desperate shot at the only deer he had seen, at a full run at great distance. The lump in his back pocket, shoved down below his handkerchief, would be his alone to remember.

Responding finally to dinner announcements from downstairs, the old man stood and reached to touch the bullet. About him, on all sides, hung the heads of deer, their polished arrogant antlers spread, their eyes blank and passionless. Off to the south he could see coppery clouds boiling up over his vast acres of scrubby pastures and pumpjacks, above them the first stars of evening, while on the lawn birdlike children flitted in the coming dark.

LAMAR LOPER'S
FIRST
CASE

"HERE. Right here'll be fine. You don't want to get any closer." The older attorney had his left hand out as if he would physically restrain the younger one, the driver, from moving farther down the driveway. "These people are territorial to a degree that you'll find surprising." He sniffed. "But you *will* find it out, Loper. By and by. Yep, this'll do."

The young attorney shut off the engine and they sat looking down the steep caliche drive, veined by recent rains, that ended at a small travel trailer hunched on the edge of the bluff over the river. Heavy brush and hardwoods came right up to the drive, the canopies of the trees joining at the top so tightly that Loper had the illusion of looking at the trailer through a gun barrel. "You mean they *live* in that?"

"They eat and sleep and screw and beat and get beat senseless in there, yeah, if that's what you mean by living in it." The older man sighed deeply. "I don't know where they use the bathroom, but there ain't room enough in there for one. He probably pisses and craps off the bluff into the river. I guess she waits and goes at work or over at her mother's or off in the bushes. Damned if I know where they bathe—*if* they bathe."

"Jesus Christ, Hammond, I'd have figured that they just camped out here on weekends and lived somewhere else, in a regular trailer or a house."

"You'd have figured wrong then. Hawkins has worked that river since he was old enough to pole and paddle to afford that piece of shit you're looking at. *If* he bought it and didn't steal it somewhere and drag it in here."

"Then why doesn't he do something else, something that pays better. I mean, Jesus Christ, Hammond, if—"

"Loper, listen, and listen good to me. You're dealing with different people than you've ever dealt with before. This ain't law school, son, and it ain't Houston or Waco or Huntsville or Corsicana or even Dimebox or Cut and Shoot. These people do what their parents did and *their* parents before them, and on and on. This is East Texas *reality*, Loper, and these people, Simmie Hawkins and a couple of hundred thousand others, live in it, and they don't change—just a notch or two out of the Gorge, or maybe a notch or two deeper in it."

The young attorney looked at him. "The gorge?"

"The Gorge, boy, the Uvalde Gorge, in Africa, where Leakey and them found the remains of primitive peoples."

Loper grinned. "You mean Olduvai Gorge—Uvalde's in Texas."

Hammond spun his head and glared at him. "Whatever. What's the difference? Olduvai, Uvalde. Both are sites of prehuman peoples, only the ones in Texas, East *or* West, are still walking around, still banging their women upside the head, still beating their kids, still, in short, at just the dawn of civilization—and worse, Loper, they are still *breeding*. And we, you and me, have got to deal with them." He looked back down the narrow drive.

On their way out of Huntsville, Hammond had had him stop and idle for nearly a full minute at the four-way stop where 19 branched off east and north to Trinity and 190 headed due east toward Livingston.

"Ed McDaniels says that East Texas begins right here, that from this point on you're in the Middle Ages until you get to the Mississippi, where civilization begins again, barely. First there's—"

"Who's Ed McDaniels?" Loper asked.

"District judge. Judge McDaniels. Aw, hell, I keeping forgetting that you don't know any of these people yet. You'll learn. Good judge. Old and tough as leather, but fair. Mad as hell most of the time at the trash we bring into his court. As I was saying, the judge says that in a corridor about a hundred miles wide from here to the Mississippi there is less intelligence and more violence per pound than in any other stretch its size in the country."

Cars were honking behind them, so Loper had to move on out onto 19. Hammond told him to drive slowly, Loper supposed because he had so much to tell the young lawyer about the case they were involved in, or maybe because he was in no hurry to get to where they were going. The older attorney's eyes stared straight out past the hood of the car, as if they were following a snake.

Loper had arrived only the evening before from Houston, fresh out of the University of Houston Law School, and didn't even have an apartment yet. His clothes were at the Holiday Inn. He had planned to take a few days to find a place and settle in, then move his wife and baby up, but as he sat in Hammond's office going over the details of the job, a call had come from some desperate woman Hammond had been dealing with and off they went, a real case before he could get his breath.

A few miles outside Huntsville Hammond pulled his briefcase over from the back seat and opened it. He took out a clutch of files and after singling out a few began reading aloud to Loper from briefs and pleadings, descriptions of the parties involved, all the background material that the young attorney would need to know.

"I know you were thinking," the older attorney said, glancing at the road from time to time, "that you were off on a routine divorce case, but you'll come to see soon enough that what's routine out here in the Thicket is probably downright extraordinary to someone fresh out of law school. I mean, you've heard of domestic violence and crime in downtown Houston, but that is nothing, son, compared to what you're going to run into up here. Every son-of-a-bitch of 'm has a gun in his pocket or under his pillow, a knife in his boot, chains and clubs, claw hammers, chainsaws. They fight and claw and cut each other up, then go to church on Sunday and pray and weep and go home and start the week over, bloodying wives and kids and cousins. Crazy bastards. Animals. A divorce case down there may get passionate, people might even get hurt and killed, but out here—hell, you just got to see for yourself." He cut his eyes over at Loper. "I'm just glad it's you coming on line and not me."

"What are you going to do?" Loper asked him. "You retiring?"

"No, no, I'm moving to Austin to spend my last few years in environmental law. That's what I've always wanted to do, but, as they say, in East Texas there's a lawyer behind every tractor tire, and when I got out of law school I was so broke that I had to start at something, and Southeast Texas Legal Services sounded like a good deal. Only . . . ," his voice trailed off, "only I stayed too long, too long among people like this." He waved his hand off toward the forested roadside, where an occasional squalid shack bobbed by in a pool of junked automobiles and household garbage.

"What is it about these people that makes them so different?" Loper asked.

"Ignorance. Poverty. Unforked family trees. Field-grade sorriness—not necessarily in that order. But mostly it's because all the male children aren't killed at birth. They ought to do that, routinely, maybe keep them alive as long as they are cute and manageable, then drown them in the river, certainly no later than age fourteen; another option would be to combine castration and circumcision—that'd catch on because the doctors and midwives could add another couple of hundred to every male birth. Parents could choose: castration at birth or a drowning a bit later. They wouldn't have much trouble from the ones they let live. After the male problem was settled, they would take all the women and artificially impregnate them with sperm from carefully selected males with a proven IQ of at least eighty, and in a couple of generations East Texas would crawl right out of the Dark Ages."

Loper smiled and looked straight ahead, his eyes boring into the tunnel through the trees, his mind on his lovely young wife back in Houston and the cuddly son she was probably that very moment holding to her breast.

*   *   *

"Do you think she's in there?" Loper whispered. They had sat in the drive for more than a quarter of an hour waiting and watching, but there had been no sign of life, except for the passing of a gaunt hound from one end of the trailer to the other. He did not even turn to look at the car.

"I don't know. I guess we'd better go see, but I doubt she'd be here. She's been staying at her momma's, her and the kid." Hammond opened the door and stepped out. The hound raised his head and looked, then dropped it back down on his paws. "It's a cinch *he's* not here or he'd have been out here with a shotgun to see what we want. Besides, the truck's gone. I'll go knock, but I'm sure she's not here. Hell, you can't—" He closed the door and Loper couldn't hear the rest of what he said.

Loper got out too and walked up behind the older man as he leaned over the concrete-block and plank steps and rapped on the trailer with one knuckle, the flat, tinny sound echoing into the trees that came up on two sides of the little trailer like a dark curtain. Hammond waited a few seconds and rapped again, this time sharper. Loper thought he could see the trailer rock on its blocks.

"There's nobody here," Loper said, squinting through a window. "Let's get back in the car and wait. This place is creepy."

"Loper." Hammond had stepped to the end of the humpbacked trailer and was motioning toward the river. Loper eased up behind him and looked where he pointed. Down the steep slope of the trail that led to the brown, torpid stream a slender girl, or woman, was crouched over a pile of fish, cleaning them, throwing the heads, skin, and entrails into the water at her feet. Her arms seemed too delicate for the bruise-colored catfish, whose skin she removed with a pair of pliers. She was wearing a nondescript dress that fell over her body and onto the ground. Her hair, with gleaming auburn speckles where the thin rays of morning sun broke through the canopy of trees, cascaded over her shoulders and onto her chest; from time to time she tossed her head back and shook her face free. The two men stood quietly watching from the bluff.

"Is that her?" Loper finally whispered.

"Yeah. That's her. She hasn't heard us. He's just about beat her deaf. Hammond took a step to the very edge of the bluff, motioning Loper to stay back. "Jeanne Ann, that you?" he yelled down the slope.

The girl dropped the fish she was cleaning and lifted her head, cocking it to the side, like a little bird, intent. When Hammond yelled again, louder, she spun around on her heels, hand flinging the pliers down and scooping up a long-bladed knife in one motion. She aimed the knife toward Hammond's voice, but Loper couldn't tell whether she had seen them. She was swinging her head from right to left as if searching for the sound, all the while keeping the knife thrust forward. "Who is it?" she shrilled. "What do you want?"

"Jeanne Ann, Jeanne Ann, calm down." Hammond had moved one foot over the edge of the bluff and onto the trail, but he did not step down toward her. "It's me, Donald Hammond, with the legal service. You know me. We've got some papers." He had his arms spread in appeal. "Will you come on up?"

The girl laid the knife down on the newspaper the cleaned fish were stacked on and stood. She leaned down to the water, scooped up a handful of sand, and scrubbed her hands vigorously, wiped them dry on her dress, and climbed slowly up the trail, her head bent forward as if she were following the path for the first time.

When she had come close enough, Hammond reached forward and offered a hand, which she refused, taking a long, undignified step onto the edge of the bluff. She wiped her hands one more time and pointed down the trail. "I was cleaning fish that he brought in this morning. I didn't hear you." She hesitated. "I don't hear good anymore, you know, don't see real good either." She turned then and shook her hair back. "Who's he?"

She was looking at Loper. Her hair had fallen back into two streams onto her shoulders, her face rising out like something breaking from the surface of a dark river. Loper stared quietly into the eyes that rose to his.

* * *

"Eighteen separate breaks?" Loper stared over at him. "The face doesn't have eighteen bones *in* it, Hammond." The older attorney had been reading from the file, describing the trip the girl had made to the hospital after her last beating. "And how many stitches?"

"Something over two hundred," Hammond answered. "He really worked on her. Beat her with a Goddamned ratchet wrench. He found eighteen bones to break, or *made* eighteen. The doctor said eighteen. Then the cretin sliced her up with a pocket knife or a fillet knife, something damned sharp. Whipped the kid with a fish stringer, one of those wire ones, cut his legs and back up bad. Pocked both of 'm with cigarettes."

"And they let the girl go back to him, with the kid?" Loper winced as a logtruck passed them. Pieces of bark flew off the bouncing bed and pelted the windshield.

"Yep," said Hammond, "put Simmie in jail for one night, then turned him loose and sent him home—because she wouldn't press charges, and because he didn't actually *kill* her. Hell, man, she told me she didn't want to cause him any trouble. She just wants to get herself and the kid away from him."

Eighteen breaks. Over two hundred stitches. *Dear God,* Loper thought, his chin on the steering wheel, his eyes boring into the tunnel of trees, his mind on the exquisite face of his wife back in Houston.

He stared at the face before him, thrust up out of the divided streams of auburn hair like a tumbled, fractured stone. Where there should have been smooth white, marvelously curved skin aglow with youth there was a hard, angular representation of a human face, like something a child might draw, with the colors all wrong, deep bruises abounding, the features askew, angry puckered scarlet zipperings running down one cheek and up the other, across the forehead and down one side of her nose. As if she'd been pieced together by a child, by someone who didn't know what a nineteen-year-old woman ought to look like.

"My name," he said, extending his hand, "is Lamar Loper, and I'm going to be your new lawyer."

She tentatively reached her hand out to his. "Jeanne Ann." Her fingers were cold and thin, but astonishingly strong-feeling. Loper stared at her eyes, so passionless, dead, as if they looked nowhere at all, as if they expected nothing of anyone, as if they belonged to someone who had resigned herself forever to a travel trailer perched over a dark, sluggish river and a man of infinite cruelty.

"Read that again about the boy." They were well north of Trinity now, and the road seemed more and more narrow as Loper drove, the trees closing in, their canopies sometimes joining from both sides. The sun swung first right, then left, as if confused. "The injuries."

Hammond cleared his throat and took his eyes off the road. "Well, the doctor said that he had little half-moon shapes all over his back and legs and stomach where the wire loops of that stringer cut in. Said, and here I quote, 'The boy looked as if he had red scales all over him.' And there were a couple dozen cigarette burns."

"Jesus Christ, Hammond. And they let the boy go back?"

"They let him go back with her, to her momma's, but that redneck bastard went and got her yesterday and worked on her again. She called this morning from her momma's, which is where I hope she is. The boy is off at an uncle's house."

"Nobody can stop him?"

"Not unless we can, which is doubtful," Hammond answered. His eyes were back on the road, turning from time to time to follow a shack until it disappeared behind them. "We can't do much with him, but this restraining order may keep him off until we can get her legally free of him and located some damned where out of this Godforsaken river bottom."

"The sheriff can't do anything?"

"Loper, the Law really doesn't do much good out here. The sheriff can do just so much 'without the papers,' as they say. Now maybe he can do something, but I don't know. He hates coming out here almost as much as I do. And, hell, by the time he gets around to serving the official papers, Hawkins might kill her. I just hope what we've got here will slow him down long enough for the sheriff or a constable to get to him. You just don't—Loper, you just haven't seen enough yet. You just don't know."

"Seems like someone could reason with him."

"You reckon so, huh? If religion won't do it, and appeal to family, and threats of jail, there's nothing left but offering him money not to beat them. Hell, I know you're filled with slobbering idealism, boy, but you just don't know what these animals are like. You can't reason with them. And you can't just kill them. You just have to try to keep the women and kids out of their way."

Loper shook his head and drove on, his mind far to the south.

"Where's Simmie, Jeanne Anne?" Hammond asked, reaching out an arm to move her away from the edge of the bluff. "Off in the truck?"

She turned from Loper. "No, off in the river, running lines. The truck's over at Jefferson's, broke down. One of his buddies brought us over here."

"Jefferson's Store," Hammond explained to Loper. "Back in there a few miles." He pointed up the river. "When's he coming back?"

"I heard him a little while ago crank up and move, so he ain't got much left to run." She turned and looked down the slope toward the brown river. "It won't be long."

"Arright," Hammond said, "we got the papers here that ought to keep him off of you. It's a restraining order, signed by a judge, and he can't touch you or the boy or anything y'all own until the court settles all this."

She shook her hair to the side and looked at him. "Them's papers. He'll burn paper, that's all. Maybe if you'd brought a shotgun . . . How come the sheriff ain't with you? You shoulda brought him to serve them papers."

"Not necessary. We can deliver them," Loper said, watching the river churning below him, eddying and surging, as brown as a cesspool. The fish lay in two piles, one dark, the other pink in the climbing sun, which had broken over the bluff in what seemed to him one blinding bound. He pointed to the fish. "Should you do something with them? Maybe put them on ice?"

The girl looked down toward the river. "You ain't got to tell me about fish. We ain't got any ice. They'll keep till he gets back. They've kept longer."

"Does he make you do that?" Loper pointed again to the fish.

"Of course he makes me do that. You figger I want to? I got to go to work at noon, and I got no way to get this fish smell off me but to jump in the river, and you can see how clean that is. I ain't got no way to go to Momma's to take a show'r." She held out her thin arms to him. "I'm sick of this, I *hate* it, but unless—" She hunched her shoulders and put her head between her hands. "Unless you can get him off of me I'll be cleaning fish for him forever and going to work stinking and coming home and getting beat up, and Jimmy getting whipped too." She jerked her head up and glared at Loper. "But this ain't nothing much to you, is it? Just a job. You figger *you* can do what Mr. Hammond can't? He's leaving, and you're all I got between me and Simmie? Jesus, you're littler and not no older than Simmie—he'll chew you up and spit you out. You gon' give him some *papers?*" Her voice twisted into a shrill, haunting laugh that echoed all about the three of them on the bluff.

Hammond had been looking off down the river. He blinked his eyes rapidly, then turned to Loper. "I guess you'd better get her out of here, Lamar. I think I can hear his motor. Take her to the car and I'll meet him. It'd be better if he didn't see her. I'll see if he'll take the papers." Hammond spoke slowly, wiped his hand across his mouth, and shrugged. He seemed now much older, stooped, his face gray, like a very old man resigned to an unpleasantness that he had finally decided was his alone to face.

Loper felt the hard fingers of the girl close on his arm, pulling at him like a drowning woman. He glanced at the river, then at Hammond. "No." He drew the word out. "Let me have the papers and I'll give them to him. You take her to the car with you."

"Lamar—" The older attorney stood looking at the river a few seconds, his face turned toward the rising sound of the motor, then went to the car and took out a folder.

Loper walked the girl to the car. He reached into the back seat and removed his briefcase, opened it, and dropped in the folder. The girl slid past him onto the rear seat.

The road was rougher now and narrower, and Loper could see up ahead where asphalt gave way to caliche. They had been quiet for miles. Loper smiled over at Hammond. "You know, I may be young and naive, but I just believe that these people can be dealt with, and I wouldn't be here if I didn't believe it. And I won't be here long if I get to believing that I can't do the job."

Hammond grunted and reached into his shirt pocket, removing an open package of cigarettes and extracting one expertly with a shake of his hand. "Yeah, I thought like that once myself." He lit the cigarette and wreathed his head with smoke. "Long time ago." The blue smoke streamed across onto Loper's side and out his window vent. "Back when I had dew on me. It won't take long out here for you to dry off, Lamar. Just keep your limitations in mind."

The car rumbled onto caliche. "How much farther?" Loper asked, clenching his eyes from the stinging smoke.

"Go till you run out of sunlight or hit the river," Hammond said. "Then you'll be there."

The boat came slowly up the current on the near side, the motor idling from time to time as the man running it stopped to check sethooks dangling from limbs or long poles jabbed in the bank. Loper still could not fully see him, but through holes in the trees and brush a shock of hair would appear, or a flash of shirt sleeve, a lean arm would streak out like a snake and jerk up a line, drop it, and pull back into the curtain of green. Loper stood silently watching, his hand tightening and loosening on the briefcase handle. Then the boat broke out into the open, veered to the right, and ground into the muddy bank, and Loper looked for the first time into the green eyes of Simmie Hawkins.

Hawkins slung a stringer of catfish onto the bank and stood up, legs spread to balance himself. "Who the hell are you?" he asked Loper, who had taken a couple of steps down the path.

Loper shifted the briefcase to his left hand and held the other one up, like an Indian greeting a stranger. "Name's Loper. I'm from the legal service. Think we can talk?"

Hawkins put one foot on the metal seat in front of him and leaped to the bank. "About what? I don't remember ordering no lawyer." He was tall and skinny, snuff-colored, and his face was sharp like some kind of animal's—Loper couldn't decide what kind. His arms were sinewy and roped with veins.

"About the restraining orders in my bag here." Loper tapped the briefcase.

"Shiiit," Hawkins sneered, his lips pulling back to reveal teeth that to Loper looked precisely as he had suspected they would. "Papers ain't nothing to me. That woman's mine and she ain't got no say in it and neither have you. Why don't you get on back up that path before I forget how nice a feller I am? Where the hell's she at anyhow?" He looked at the fish still lying uncleaned on the newspaper. "Them damned fish ain't finished."

"Why don't we go into the trailer, Simmie, and talk about this, like gentlemen? What can it hurt?" He extended a hand to Hawkins, who brushed past him and clambered onto the bluff. He stood there a few seconds looking down on Loper.

"All right, then, come on and let's talk. Don't hurt y'self getting up here. I might have to hire myself a li-bility lawyer to defend me." His face cracked into a sidelong grin.

The inside of the trailer was tight and dark, even with the curtains pulled back on the side facing the river. There was a small range at one end, wedged in between slim cabinets, an apartment-size refrigerator beside it, and on top of the refrigerator a foot-square television. How they got a signal this far out, Loper could not imagine—he had seen no antenna. Hell, it probably didn't work. There was a combination bed/couch right across from the door, and, to his surprise, at the opposite end from the kitchen a bathroom of some sort. He could see a commode and miniature sink. A little sleeping bag was rolled up beside the couch, for the child, he supposed, or for the girl. In front of the couch two lawn chairs faced each other, separated by a coffee table made of a board and two concrete blocks.

"Well, set down, Mr. Law," Hawkins said, sprawling back on the couch. "I'd offer you a beer, if I had one, and if you was *my* lawyer. As it is, I don't give a damn if you die of thirst."

Loper settled into one of the lawn chairs and brought his eyes slowly around from the blank television screen to Hawkins, noting beyond the man's head the solid line of dark trees on the other side of the river. He studied the face for a few seconds before speaking. The briefcase lay on his lap.

"I've got these papers with me, Hawkins, restraining orders, that you need to take a look at." He unsnapped the flap of the briefcase and sprang the top open enough to get the folder out. He opened the file and spread the orders on the table, tapping them with his index finger. "You know what these are all about, I suppose."

"I don't *care* what they are, but I reckon I know," Hawkins replied.

"They outline what you cannot do while the divorce proceeding is underway—like visit your wife or the child or venture onto the premises where she's staying or touch her or the kid or bother anything that belongs to her or the child, or take anything from the trailer—anything at all—until everything's settled in court." Loper looked straight into Hawkins's eyes as he spoke.

Hawkins reached onto the counter for a cigarette and lit it, sending a billow of smoke toward Loper. He picked up the papers and held them over in the light from the window. Reading slowly, his eyes following a finger down the lines, he grunted from time to time, smiled once, then laid the orders back down on the table. "Look like you ol' boys done tied me up good, don't it? Can't touch my family, can't move nothing at all out of the trailer, just can't do much of nothing, can I?" His voice was rising as he sneered. "And y'all gon' give'r most of the estate, I guess, what y'all don't get for fees."

Loper smiled, still staring directly into his eyes. "That's right. It'll all be settled in court. We're public lawyers, though, and don't have to collect fees." He pulled another form out of the briefcase. "I'd like you to sign that you've read all this."

"You're crazy as hell. Divorce don't mean nothing to me. That's just more paper. And them orders sure as hell don't mean nothing. I ain't got to sign *nothing.*"

"No," Loper said quietly, "by law you don't have to sign that you've read the papers. You are bound by them, whether you sign them or not. The sheriff will be out in a couple of days to serve the official orders, but these will do, now that you are aware that they exist. But I want you to *sign* that you've read them."

"And people in hell want ice-tea. I ain't signing shit. You want to *make* me sign'm?" He stood up, fists clenched, and glared down at Loper. "I seen that old fart Hammond out there. He gon' help you make me?"

Loper smiled up at him. "Are you going to whip me, Simmie, like you did Jeanne Ann and your little boy? Are you going to break more bones in my face than I knew I had? Are you going to thrash me with a fish stringer, burn me with cigarettes? All of the above?" He was staring Hawkins straight in the eyes.

"Just how the hell would you stop me? I can whup you and that old fart—"

"Easy as whipping a girl and little boy, huh?" Loper slid his hand into the satchel.

Hawkins yanked his watch off and pitched it onto the counter beside him. "I'm going to tear your face off, smartass."

"Boy, I'm going to be real pissed if you make me ruin my bag."

"Whu—"

"Just shut up a minute, Simmie, and sit down and lean a little bit toward my bag and see if can you hear all the little ratchets and springs when I cock the pistol that's in there. An S & W Mountain Revolver, .44 magnum, a *bear* gun, Simmie, and I'd just as soon not blow the bottom of my bag off in the process of blowing *your* bag off."

"You're bluffing." He was glaring at Loper, but he stood motionless.

"Come on, Simmie, lean down just a little bit and listen to it cock. All stainless steel, a beautiful gun. You'd love it. It can blow your head and the side of this trailer off with one shot."

The boy stepped back and stumbled into the corner of the couch. "Man, you're crazy. If you got a gun in that bag, you're breaking the law."

"Simmie, you little redneck bastard, if it weren't for animals like you, guns would be novelties in this country, like maces and tomahawks and spears, fit for hanging on walls and reminiscing about. Smith and Wesson and Ruger and Colt would be making auto parts and condom machines. Men wouldn't have pistols in their dashboxes, stuffed into coat pockets, and women wouldn't be packing Lady Smiths. You little vermin, you slime trackers— you are the cause of most of the violence and suspicion and fear that pervades this country. You ignorant, low-life cretins." Loper, his hand still in the satchel, had risen to his feet now, towering over Hawkins, hunched on the couch. He held the satchel in front of him.

"You can't treat me like this, man," Hawkins sputtered. "You're part of the Law. You can't hold a gun on a man in his own house."

Loper pressed the satchel to the boy's chest. "But I can if you live in a *trailer*, you ignorant asshole. That's state law, Simmie, which you probably need to learn a little more of. I'm holding this gun on you because it's one of the few ways of getting your attention. And you had better damned well listen to me."

"You mean a trailer's different? You can hold a gun on a man that lives in a trailer? I never heard that before. That's the *law?*"

"You want me to quote you the chapter and verse, boy? That river out there couldn't handle what you don't know about the law." He was forcing him deeper into the cushions of the couch.

Hawkins shook his head. The challenge was gone from his face now. His lips were pulled back into a tight line, almost bloodless, and his eyes reflected what Loper knew was the first flickering of genuine fear.

The satchel balanced in his left hand, right hand still deep inside it, Loper began talking softly. "Simmie, my name is Lamar Loper, and I'm from Natchez, Mississippi, and I come from a long line of distinguished military leaders and politicians and patriarchs. My people still have money and power and arms longer than any Law you know."

He knew he was becoming too poetic, but his blood was moving now, charging him with strange exhilaration. "You ever heard of the Dixie Mafia, Simmie?"

The boy nodded, his Adam's apple pumping.

"You probably know something of their power. You know that they can go and get things done where the Law doesn't dare to tread." Jesus, he needed to tone it down. But the boy looked like a cornered animal, his eyes an almost pure white.

"I've got an uncle who's in the DM, Simmie, and when I need a favor outside the law, I just call him. He's got a lieutenant named Jesus—and he pronounces it Jee-zus, not Hay-soos—that's killed more people than you've got brain cells, which probably isn't a good comparison, but the point is that he is Mister Violence Himself. And, Simmie, I know Jesus personally, and he likes me and will do anything for me."

The boy was swallowing now and then and staring, unblinking, into Loper's eyes.

"Jesus has one favorite tactic for convincing people, Simmie, and it's about as cruel a punishment as I've heard of. He cuts off men's uvulas. Just like cutting a calf. You ever seen a calf cut, Simmie?" The boy nodded. "Just like that, only he does it slow, so that it hurts, hurts like hell, he says. Does it with his pocket knife. Simmie, you ever heard a man talk who's had his uvula cut off?" Hawkins shook his head. "He sounds like a sheep, Simmie, like a female sheep. Pitiful and whining and puny, just like a female sheep. And, Simmie, it don't grow back—there's just an awful scar where it used to hang. He ble-e-e-eats the rest of his life."

Loper knew that the boy didn't know a uvula from a testicle and that there wasn't a book on the place that he could look the word up in, even if he could spell it close enough to find it. He wasn't satisfied, though, and he knew that he wouldn't be for a while yet. He leaned and pushed the curtain aside to see what Hammond was doing with the girl. They were still sitting in the car.

He returned to the attack. "Simmie, you are just a little snot-nosed white trash, ignorant piece of subhuman filth, not worth a

bullet from the .44 aimed at you. While other families were trying to get themselves and their offspring educated, their living
conditions improved, nature was doing her damnedest just trying
to get your family's eyebrows up off their cheekbones far enough
that they could at least see how to bait a trotline.

"Now, you listen to me, Simmie. Court talk doesn't scare you.
I know that. And getting your ass whipped doesn't scare you. But
let me tell you something, you little white-trash animal, if I get
my uncle to send Jesus over here from South Mississippi to handle
this problem, you're going to suffer more than you can imagine.
Jesus tortures with exquisite pleasure. He says that he experiences
rapture, *rapture*, when he whacks off a uvula."

He could have ordered the boy to eat a pint of fishhooks now
and he'd have done it, but something at some savage level goaded
him on.

"And, Simmie, if I ask them to, Jesus and his boys will poison
the Trinity and kill every damned catfish from Fort Worth to the
Gulf and you'll have to leave the river and get a job outside the
Thicket, where the sun is, Simmie, where there's light and civilization and decent people who speak real language and use com-
modes and eat with forks and spoons. You wouldn't like it out
there, Simmie.

"And, yeah, Simmie, she's going get most of the estate, as you
call it." Loper cast his eyes quickly about the trailer. "She's going
to get whatever you can sell this trailer for, and she's going to get
your boat and truck and most of your fishhooks, boy."

He drew his hand from the briefcase and removed his wallet,
noting how Hawkins seemed not even aware that the hand was
no longer in the bag. He pulled out a dollar bill, tore it in half,
and handed one half to Hawkins. "You keep this half of a dollar."

Hawkins stared at it, turning it over and over. "What's it for?"

"It's to have if Jesus comes for you. He'll ask for the half a dollar bill that matches this one." Loper held out his half. "You don't
have it, Simmie, he'll probably just kill you." He thrust out his
hand as if he held a knife and flicked it to the left and right.
"After he cuts off your uvula."

"But what's it for? What does it mean?" The boy was holding the piece of paper as if it were part of a snake he'd picked up in the road.

"It doesn't *mean* anything, Simmie. It's just to have if Jesus has to come for you. If you have it, it'll mean you believe me and believe in him, and that'll mean something to him. If you don't have it, there's no telling what he'll do. But I'll tell you this, I wouldn't put that stack of festering catfish down there against your uvula if he does come."

Hawkins sat in the dark trailer staring at the half a dollar bill in his stringy fingers. "I never met no lawyer like you before," he muttered.

"You'd better not touch Jeanne Ann or that boy again or violate any part of these restraining orders, or you'll see me again. And you sign this form for me." He handed the boy his pen. Hawkins's hand shook as he reached and took it, lowered it to the line that Loper pointed to, and laboriously scrawled his name.

"You get somebody to read through these carefully with you, Simmie, and don't let me hear anything about you until the court has settled all this." He took back the pen, folded the form and stuck it into his briefcase, turned slowly around, and with a faint smile stepped out of the trailer into bright day.

"It'd be one thing," Hammond was saying as the car settled softly onto asphalt, headed south, "if we had just managed to get away from there with our lives, maybe bleeding just a little, fishing poles sticking out our asses or something, and glad that was as bad as it got. I could believe that. I could even believe it if you had chickened out and just flung the papers down that slope at him and hauled ass to the car. But I just cannot fathom this: the papers hand-delivered and a signed receipt." He held the form out before him like some sacred religious document.

Loper had one wrist hooked casually over the top of the steering wheel. He looked over at Hammond. "Well, I told you that these people could be reasoned with. You're just used to the old ways. Today you got to finesse, stroke, cajole, maybe beg a little, if you have to. Like dealing with kids, really, like—"

"Come on, Loper. How'd you do it? You had to use religion, family, money, something more than just reason and flattery and begging."

Loper smiled. "Well, yeah, family did come up. We talked a little bit about family, and I brought up Jesus—"

"I knew it, damn it," Hammond roared. "Jesus, family! Hell, that won't last till our dust settles. He'll cut right through the woods to her momma's house and get her before we can get back to the office. We should have brought her on out with us, her and the boy."

Loper shook his head. "No, I don't think so. I think his attitude change will last. It wasn't just family and Jesus."

Hammond hooted and slammed the dash with his open hand. "Goddamn, boy, what's left? You sure didn't threaten him with the Law. That hasn't worked since he was twelve, if then, and you didn't threaten him physically, little as you are." He reached over and pinched Loper's thin, pale arm. He slammed the dash again. "Ho, ho, now I'll bet I got it—you gave him money, didn't you? You *paid* him to leave her alone. Jesus, you are more naive than I first believed." He swung his head from side to side slowly.

Loper cleared his throat and smiled. "Some money changed hands, yeah, but—"

"Won't last half a day, not half a damned day. You sound like a damned missionary. Preach to'm, plead with'm, give'm money, and they'll agree to anything, until you pack up and leave. By morning they'll be roasting their children over a fire made of your Sunday-school books and bibles."

"It's a civilized world now, Hammond. They teach us different tactics from what you learned. You have to appeal to their common sense. You've got to have faith in people, Hammond," Loper said, speeding up now that they were on a widening, smooth road. The sun was higher and broke easily through the tree canopy overhead, sprinkling the asphalt, then submerging them in an almost dazzling ocean of light as the car glided softly along at what seemed to Loper vaguely like the beginning of a most promising career.

THE MAN
WHO WOULD BE
GOD

Against the western sky the towering white house seemed as anomalous to the two cowboys as the moon sometimes did hovering in its distant beauty and peace above land that, though they would never think of leaving it, was as austere as anyone could imagine. On the cat-walk that ran along the ridge of the second story, widening to an observation platform at one gable, a solitary figure in white eased along until, having come at last to the point where he stopped every rainless day they could remember over the past four years, he stood long and stared at the sparse rangeland, scattered with sage and mesquite, that stretched out to the darkening hills.

"There's Jehovah, right on schedule," one of the cowboys said, not exactly to the other one, but as much in his direction as any; he punctuated the statement with a sigh and squirt of tobacco juice that was drawn into the dust almost before it had finished splattering at his feet.

"Yep. Looking over Paradise one more time before he puts the world to bed again."

"You know, Earl," the first one confided, leaning his chair toward his listener, "there was a time I might have felt sorry for that poor son-of-a-bitch, crazy as he is, lonely as he is—but not no more. He chose it that way."

"Yep. He chose it."

To have passed Bob Billings on the streets of any of the nearby one-horse West Texas towns in the days when he was growing into his father's vast holdings in land, oil, and banking, a stranger would have thought him merely an odd-shaped little man destined to do no more or less in this life than get by. He was short, slender, red-faced, his eyes a moody brown, and the hump in his back already swelling out the back of his shirt, though he was still a young man. Rich as the family was, beyond all imagining in a land where oil and gas had made many a man wealthy, Billings dressed in the same dark suit each day until it frayed and tattered to the point that apparently he felt it necessary to buy a new one, exactly like the old, from a J. C. Penney store in San Antonio. Or so the story went, one of the many about Bob Billings, who, since he came out with his mother only after the old man had built his dynasty, seemed not to have any origins at all: He was simply there one morning in his father's bank in Divot, a taciturn young man with no social life who occupied space for a few hours each day and was gone.

Whether by choice or under the direct orders of his father, himself an eccentric and notoriously silent, the son served as a junior bank officer and general flunky to the old man until the senior Billings died, whereupon he sold the bank and other family enterprises in nearby towns and retreated to the great white house that sat on the Double Star, one of the many cattle spreads—bought or foreclosed on or won in a card game—that his father had owned. From there he ran the family empire, the mother long since having died and Bob an only child. What his total holdings were, no one around Divot knew; or if anyone knew, he had no proof, though wild were the figures that the old men threw around at twilight sitting along Main Street waiting for night to fall and the card games to begin. It was a standard joke that he could buy Texas itself and have enough left over to put a down payment on Europe. Whatever the worth of his inherited wealth, Bob Billings kept it to himself in his lonely castle at the Double Star.

After his father's death, Billings lived alone out there, apparently neither needing nor wanting friends or lovers. He kept a handful of cowboys, who lived in a long bunkhouse a few hundred yards from the main house, and one Mexican woman to do the cooking and washing. His father had left a capable cadre of lawyers and financiers to advise his son, and speculation was that Billings had simply accepted them as they were and the empire continued to operate smoothly, as if nothing had changed. An occasional official-looking car boiled up the dirt driveway to the house, sat not even long enough for the engine to cool, then boiled back out again. The Mexican housekeeper never left the house and might as well have been mute for all the light she shed on the mystery of Billings; and the cowboys, who saw him very seldom, then only at a distance, were instructed by a foreman from another of the ranches, a man who, if he knew much about what went on at the house, was reluctant to talk about it with them. How he got instructions was not clear.

It was one of the cowboys, Nathan Warwick, who finally, in a late-night poker game after he had lost all he had brought to town with him and was close to slobbering drunk, let slip the seed of a Billings story that would swell to the dimension of legend over the next few years. Fluent enough in Spanish and more than capable with women, Nathan had yielded at last to the gnawing in his loins and talked the Mexican housekeeper into bedding with him. She was not a pretty woman, was in fact short and heavy and not so very young, but she was *handy*, as Nathan put it, and she did have what all women, he thanked the Lord, had. After much entreaty, she agreed to share it with him.

After a few weeks of lovemaking about the place—more often than not on a blanket under some mesquite bush late in the night, but certainly never where anyone might stumble upon them—Nathan and Rosanna reached an agreement whereby she would leave the back door unlocked and Nathan would ease in through the mudroom and kitchen and into Rosanna's room, on the bottom floor adjoining the kitchen. He always waited an hour after he saw the lights go out on the second floor, usually somewhere between ten and eleven. By then the other cowboys were asleep or off in town. Not that he cared what they might think—not one of them would refuse to fuck Rosanna or the mule she rode in on—but Nathan wanted to take no chances on Billings finding out about the affair.

Sometimes after making love, especially if there was no range work the next day and Nathan could sleep late, they lay and talked long into the night. He tried a couple of times to get her to talk about "The Man," as she called him, but Rosanna steadfastly refused to bring Billings into their conversations, preferring instead to dwell on her childhood days in Fuente. Her stories were good ones, nostalgic and pleasant to the ear, so Nathan did not push: He knew that sooner or later she would talk about him.

"He said what?" Hands fell to the table in unison when Nathan blurted it out. Jimmy Scarr was leaning across with his mouth open in front of Nathan's stubble-shadowed face.

"That's what she said. When she finally started talking to me about him."

"He wants to be God?" Scarr took another long swig from his beer. "He told some Meskins that he wants to be their God?"

"Yeah, Jimmy, their God." Nathan took another shot. "But look, I ought not to be talking about this. I reckon I better get on back out there."

"Bullshit," Walter Benson shouted, rising to his feet. "Here we been wondering about that crazy son-of-a-bitch for years and we find out somebody knows something about him—you figger we gon' let you get out of here without telling us?" He reached over and pushed Nathan down in his chair. The other members of the game nodded. "We ain't being unreasonable, Nathan. We let you walk away from this table lots of times with winnings that we never had no chance to take back, but you ain't taking this pot out with you. You ain't got to work tomorrow, so set here and share it with us. Whiskey's free." He turned to the others. "We buying his booze."

So with the cluster of men gathered around him and the night wearing away to morning, Nathan slugged down shot after shot of whiskey and told Rosanna's story.

"That particular night the moon was out real bright and we decided that we'd go walking . . ."

"This was after you'd buggered the old whale, huh?"

"Jimmy, you shut up," someone shot back. "Get on with it, Nathan."

"Well, we slipped out the back door and walked out to the tank by the windmill—you know where it's at—and set down awhile and watched the shadows of the blades turning in the dust."

"This old boy's a poet."

"Jimmy," a voice said from the smoke of the table, "you been told to shut up. Now if you don't want to find out how quick that beer bottle of yours can get from your asshole with teeth in it to the one that ain't got teeth, you better shut the one with teeth."

"Well," Nathan continued, "the next morning being Sunday and neither one of us having to get up early, we set there a couple of hours talking about nothing in particular when I just out and asked her what was going on at the main house. There'd been a steady stream of Mexicans coming to the back door lately, knocking and going in and coming back out, sometimes with stuff in their arms, sometimes not. They'd get back on their jackasses and head over toward that squatter settlement—you know where it is—down on the river."

"You mean that wetback camp?" somebody asked.

Nathan nodded and took a slug from the bottle that sat beside his glass. "Well, it's more than that. Lots of them folks has been out there for years, families of 'm, but we got ideas that they let wetbacks stay there on their way over to San Antonio."

"We don't care about that damned wetback camp, Nathan," Jimmy Scarr snapped. "Get on with the story about Billings wanting to play God."

"Aw-right, aw-right. Them Mexicans had been coming around the house a good bit lately and I just wondered what was happening, so I asked her. Well, I could tell right off that it was something that she didn't particularly want to talk about, but the moon was nice and we was nipping from some tequila and the next day being Sunday, we could sleep late. I leaned over and nuzzled on her ear some, and she broke down and told the story." He lifted the bottle again and drank deeply, winced, belched, and stared across the table into the haze. "You sure you got time for this tonight? I'm awful tired, and I'm getting fuzzy-headed."

"We got the time, Nathan," a voice came back. "You just tell the story. Somebody get him another bottle. It's on me."

"OK. Here she goes. Now Billings, who hadn't said a word to Rosanna except for telling her to find his boots or get his brace—bet y'all didn't even know the little fart wears a back brace—all the time his daddy was alive and not much more since he died, come to her room one night. She sleeps real light anyway, so she heard his feet hit the floor and the boards creak all the way as he come from his room down to hers. He knocked and called out to her, asking if she was asleep, which she pretended to be for a while—hell, she was afraid that he'd been so woman-starved for so long that he finally couldn't stand it no longer and had come down for the only human female flesh within twenty miles, except for what was out at the settlement.

"But he wouldn't go away, just kept on knocking and calling for her until finally she acted like she had woke up and she told him to come in. She never got up, never turned on the light, so he groped into the room and over to her bed and set down beside her, not saying nothing, just breathing real deep like something was troubling him. And when he started talking to her, Spanish, of course, since she don't know enough English to call a dog, in a low, mournful, faraway voice, she just figgered he was having a heart attack or something, and his daddy not dead a year yet. He pulled his legs up on the bed and laid down beside her and put one of his hands on her shoulder. Well, she had it figgered where the next hand was going, so she tightened herself up like an armadillo and waited. But it never come. He just went on talking and rubbing her shoulder.

"He talked about how his life had been, how he had always been lonely and unloved, how people feared and respected him because of his father's wealth, and now because of his own. He talked about how he could buy airplanes or boats and crews to run them and go anywhere in the world and buy anything he wanted, exotic islands, even small nations, if he wanted to. Told about how miserable he was with all that wealth, and—"

"God," Jimmy Scarr said, "I sure would hate to have to suffer like that, but, as the saying goes, somebody's got to do it."

"And how all he really wanted was to be on the Double Star and have his own people to love and to love him. And that's where he told her that he wanted to be God, not to everybody— any fool knew that wouldn't work—but to a few simple, hard-working, deserving people, like them out at the settlement."

"Well, I'll be damned," a voice sighed from the smoke.

So the story went round as the sun rose on Divot that day— intruding into every corner, every household, like a fresh burst of gospel that, though it might not promise an everlasting life of happiness, at least offered some reprieve from the doldrums of the present one—how Bob Billings proposed to serve as God to a settlement of poor Mexican farmers on the back side of the Double Star.

Rarely numbering more than six families, some twenty-five to thirty people ranging in age from a couple of months to over seventy, the inhabitants of the Mexican settlement, which was known by no name other than The Settlement to outsiders, stopped in a bend of the Frio River one evening after the long trek from the Mexican border and, finding themselves too tired to move on, simply stayed. Poor and uneducated, but determined to make some sort of go of it in the U.S., they elected to enjoy the relative security of the river, where they found that if they kept a low profile no one would trouble them, if indeed anyone ever found them there. They knew from the fences they had crossed and the occasional signs along the way that they were on someone's property, as if any of them could have doubted that anyway, this being America, but the fact that there were no roads near and no railroad tracks and power poles offered the promise of relative isolation. They were farmers by chance and choice and had never known anything but subsistence, had never expected more. There was water to be had for the carrying, and they could manage to feed themselves; each family had set aside a few pesos and dollar bills for the few trips to small towns nearby, reached by circuitous routes so that no one would know exactly where they had come from.

Here, if they could remain unmolested, the farmers might go on growing a few things and running the handful of scrub cattle they had found along the way, their wives and younger children helping with the farming and the older children making their way, if they wished, to San Antonio or Austin or Houston, where there were jobs to be had that would put something in their pockets as well as their stomachs. They knew that word would get back that the settlement was there, that cousins and friends and dark strangers would be dropping in to spend the night or eat a meal, and they knew as well that Anglos would learn of the place and, sooner or later, the landowner. But until they were found out and made to move, they would live out their simple lives in the little settlement by the river.

The shacks, a pitiful handful, were constructed of discarded materials that they had carried or dragged in behind burros from wherever they had found them: mostly tin and barn timbers and fence posts from abandoned buildings and fence lines between the Mexican border and the Double Star. They had no real windows, only openings in the tin sides over which flaps of tin could be dropped when the weather was cold or wet enough to require it; the doors were likewise made of sheets of tin framed with planks. Dreadfully hot in the summer and miserably cold in the winter, the shacks were at best, as Rosanna told Nathan, fit for pigs to live in.

It was an impoverished existence, yet no worse, certainly, than they had had it back in Mexico, and at least here they had the opportunity to raise their children with the promise that they could, if they wished, move on to better things, and here what they did earn they kept, untaxed by any government or land-owner. They lived an isolated, somnolent life, the Mexican squatters, where they had food and water and independence. They did not enjoy much surplus—neither did they starve.

These, then, were Bob Billings's chosen people: poor, ignorant, isolated from any church, and already dependent on his good graces for the land they lived on. As he told Rosanna deep in that night of revelation, they would be the recipients of his benefi-cence and love; in return they would worship him as they would any god in whose hands they were held.

When Billings made his first trip out there, he was received with suspicion and distrust, as he told Rosanna he expected. No truck had been to the settlement before, since no roads ran to it, and this one had an Anglo in it, beside him a heavy Mexican woman; and though the bed was filled to overflowing with boxes of fruit and canned meat and dry goods, the squatters had little reason to believe that any of it was for them. They stood by their shacks as the little man, with a slight hump already rising from his far from aged back, crawled up into the bed of the truck to address them.

Billings told them that he owned the land they were living on, for farther than they could see in any direction, owned miles and miles of it, its water and soil and sky, that he owned millions of dollars and had hundreds of people working for him, that he was the richest man they would ever see. To emphasize his great wealth, he told them that he owned and lived in the big white house of the Double Star, a revelation to which they responded with a murmur of disbelief, all having heard of it or seen it.

After distributing the contents of the truck bed among the families and erecting metal signs at each end of the village with the words Nuevo Cielo in white against a green background, Billings met with the elders of the settlement in private; and though Rosanna did not hear exactly what transpired between the landowner and farmers, she learned later from one of the old men who was in the meeting that Billings had made his proposal of divine ascension. He would, over the next two years, erect permanent housing for the inhabitants of Nuevo Cielo, a name which the farmers were mirthful over at first, though they tried not to show it and offend the landowner. He would see to it that the inhabitants were clothed, fed, and given adequate medical attention. On the river a powerful pumping station was to be built to provide them with filtered water for personal use and unfiltered water for irrigation. Most importantly, Billings would supervise the construction of a church.

In return the people of Nuevo Cielo must eschew all prior religious commitments and devote themselves entirely to him, using the new church as the shrine in which they would worship him. They must pray only to him, tithe (as they could afford it) to prove their devotion, come only to him for their needs, and teach their children that Billings was the only true God there was.

There was an immediate uproar from the cluster of men—this Rosanna did hear—and a few minutes of extreme agitation before Billings got them quieted down enough to continue. He knew, he said, that they had always worshiped the God of the Catholic faith and followed the tenets of Catholicism and that this was doubtless catching them by surprise. He pointed out to them, though, where their old God had left them: poor, uneducated, isolated in the desert. He motioned to the shacks behind them. Their God had given them hovels unfit for animals to live in and forced them to walk nearly half a mile for water, which must be carried in buckets. He had not even provided them with a place to worship.

He, Billings, on the other hand, would deliver them from their misery and allow them for the first time in their lives to enjoy surplus, asking in return little by way of material reward. They would be the recipients of his generosity, he the object of their love and devotion. He told them that he would leave them to make their decision. "I will be at the big white house over there." He pointed to the north. "When you have weighed this matter and come to the answer that will mean deliverance from misery for yourselves and your children, send someone to let me know."

* * *

The people of Nuevo Cielo accepted Bob Billings's offer and he became their God. True to his word, he had a new village built, with concrete-block, tin-roofed houses, brought in electricity, and constructed a waterworks, which delivered running water to the village. Throngs of cowboys, brought in from several ranches, laid an irrigation system, built two enormous barns, and fenced in over five hundred acres for cattle pastures, which, with water, would become highly productive in a year. A social hall was added for their amusement, and a general store, from which they could purchase whatever commodities they needed at a cost that outsiders came to envy. A church with ornate external trim and elegant furnishings rose on a high point over the river, its doors facing the white house of the Double Star. In short, Nuevo Cielo became a small town, joined to a farm-to-market highway by a caliche road, a town where Bob Billings was builder, provider, and God.

"Have y'all been out there?" Nathan Warwick was drunk again and losing and eager to turn the attention of the table to something besides cards.

A murmur came from the smoke.

"Well, you ought to go. Over a hundred Mexicans live in the village now—we throwed up another couple of houses just last week. They running so many cows that we fenced in another five hundred acres and laid in some more pipes for irrigation. Hell, they got real grass growing around them houses and enough growing in the pastures that we been having to hay the stuff and store it."

"He's got y'all haying for them Meskins?" someone asked.

"All we do is help them pick it up and store it. He's got folks coming in from Pearsall to do the cutting and baling. The traffic on that little old road has picked up so much that Billings is talking about blacktopping it."

"He got y'all working the cows?"

"Well, we built some real good working pens out there, and the Mexicans can do a pretty good job theirselves, but if they need us we have to go."

"Hell of a note," Jimmy Scarr said, "whites working for them Meskins."

"Yeah," a voice came back from the smoke, "but they God's *chosen* Meskins."

"I don't reckon it matters," Nathan continued, "long's we're paid, who we work for. Them's good people, best I can tell, and they living up to their end of the bargain; hell, that place is beginning to look like it's going to be worthy of its name."

"But what about the worship part?" another cowboy asked.

"Far's I can tell, they doing that all right too. They go to the church ever Sunday and worship Billings, even made up some songs about him, hymns and such, tithe regularly, and teach their children that he's their God. When new ones come in, and, boy, the word has got out that Nuevo Cielo is there, they are made to do the same or told to move on. That's what Rosanna tells me. When them new wetbacks see what that village has got to offer, they forget purty quick about the God that they left back in Mexico and take whatever the new one has to offer. If Billings don't put some controls on things out there, he's going to have a city on his hands, with shopping centers and a damned airport."

Jimmy Scarr leaned his face out of the smoke. "Nathan, what they use for a Bible?" The group fell silent at the question.

"Well, this here's another story." Nathan took a long swallow from his bottle, which the men had gladly provided to keep the story going. "Rosanna says that Billings is writing his own."

"Jesus Christ!" someone muttered.

"Writing his own Word. Rosanna says that except for them evening trips onto the roof, wearing his white robe, he stays in that room, just stays cloistered up there—that's the way she puts it, cloistered like a monk of old—working on a Gospel for his people."

"She know what it says?" a tired voice asked.

"Naw. Can't get near that room. He won't even let her in to change the sheets, just throws them out the door once a week, and she just sets his meals down outside the door and goes and picks up the dishes later. If y'all thought he was weird before, you ain't seen nothing."

"This all sounds like blasphemy to me," an old man, a stranger in Divot said. "This here guy playing like God and writing a Gospel and all."

"If it was whites he was being God to, it *would* be," Nathan answered.

Someone asked what Billings did if there was trouble in the village. Nathan laughed and slurred, "Trouble ain't likely out there. Them old boys got too much to lose. They got their own little police force to take care of things so that Billings not only don't have to come out to see about it—he don't ever know that it happened. I tell you, they're a purty peaceful and productive lot."

Chet Brooks spoke up from the smoke: "Well, it looks like to me that anybody with Billings's money would go ahead and build a heaven and hell for'm too, long's he's doing that God thing."

"Don't need to," Nathan said. "Hell's where most of'm just come from, and they got more heaven right there than any of'm could have wanted."

Nuevo Cielo continued to prosper over the next two years, burgeoning into a virtual paradise in the desert. Its reputation spread as a place of peace and prosperity, an oasis where hungry wetbacks could spend a few days recovering from the rigors of their journey north and, if they wished, settle into the community for good. When there was trouble, it was handled quickly and firmly, with minor offenders being reprimanded and put on a probationary status, and those accused of serious crimes banished utterly from the village and told never to return.

Whether Nuevo Cielo operated at a profit or not, no one but Billings and the elders knew, but word was that within three years of its naming, the village had a positive cash flow from the sale of truck crops, hay, and cattle. A few pickups and flatbeds began showing up beside the houses, gifts from Billings, it was assumed, though outsiders did not know for certain. Even Nathan Warwick's dependable Rosanna could not determine, no matter how persistent her efforts, precisely how much money Nuevo Cielo and its inhabitants were making, or losing, and how much Billings was continuing to sink into his personal town. Rosanna did say that the long black cars had come more frequently after the village was rebuilt and the phone had rung more often, but beyond that she knew—or would say—nothing about financial matters involving Billings and the Mexicans.

Indeed, Rosanna now had little contact with the village, the early stream of peasants bearing fruit and vegetables having dried up when their tithing turned to a cash basis as Nuevo Cielo grew and prospered. The money was collected weekly and delivered by one of the elders of the church, with whom she could not seem to find common ground for communication. He brought the money to the back door in a leather bag every Monday morning just before noon and left it on the mudporch. When the Mexican was out of sight Rosanna took the bag up to Billings's room and left it outside the door.

What became of the money she was not certain, though she assumed that it was carried off to a bank by one of the men from the many black cars that came at odd hours. These silent men, dressed in dark suits and sparing not even a nod of greeting, came in without knocking, went directly to Billings's room, and after a short while came back down, got in their long black cars, and left, boiling out the dirt drive toward the highway. Where they came from and where they went, she had no idea.

"He come to her room again." The table fell silent as Nathan reached for his bottle. The night was wearing on, he was almost drunk, and the game had, as usual, been going against him.

"The first time since—" someone started.

"Yeah, the first time since the first time. Scared the hell out of her too. She was laying there looking out the window—the moon was real bright, the way it was that first night—when she heard him come down the stairs. She thought maybe he was going to the kitchen for something, since she'd heard him do that before."

"You mean even God gets hungry?" a voice asked from the smoke.

"Yep. That one does. Only this time he come to her room. He knocked real light and asked whether she was asleep. Well, hell, she didn't know what to do, so she said no, and he asked whether he could come in and talk to her. Rosanna got up and turned on the light and eased the door open. He told her to turn off the light, which she done, and he stepped through. He was dressed in that long white robe, which she said glowed like a ghost in the light from the window. It was spooky. And he was talking or singing, just a whisper, in something that wasn't English or Spanish either, some language she had never heard before, with a bunch of what she called *sharp*-sounding words, and holding a box out in front of him about this big." Nathan described a shape about the size of a boot box with his hands.

"He walked over and set down on the bed, laid the box down beside him. Rosanna was standing by the window wondering what to do. She said she was scareder this time than the first, what with the white robe and strange tongue and all. Then he leaned and put out his hand and blessed her, telling her that she was one of his chosen children too and that he loved her like the others. His hand was cold as ice where he touched her on the arm, like she'd been touched by something that wasn't even living. He pulled her onto the bed with him.

"He told her that he was finished with the Gospel—that was it in the box—and he was going to deliver it unto his people next Sunday on his return to Nuevo Cielo."

"You talking about—"

"Yeah, day after tomorrow," Nathan answered. He squinted at his watch. "Day after today. Hell, tomorrow, Sunday."

"Wouldn't mind being there for that," Jimmy Scarr said.

"That ain't all. He said he was going to walk out there, beginning at sunup."

"Bullshit!" came a voice from the smoke. "That's ten miles if it's a foot."

"Naw it ain't," Nathan corrected him, "it's eight and a half. He can do it in three hours easy."

"He going straight across or by the trail?" someone asked.

"One thing's sure," another voice answered. "He ain't going to walk on *water*."

"Rosanna never said nothing about which way he was going, only that he was going to walk, beginning at sunup. He ought to be there in time for services." He shrugged that that was all and the game broke up, with much discussion and more than one pledging that he intended to be there to witness the return of God to Nuevo Cielo.

Sunday dawned like most other deep-summer mornings on the Double Star, brightening quickly before the sun broke; a cool wind played up from Mexico to the southwest, rocking the sage and whirling the blades of the windmill. Not wishing to miss the first leg of God's trek across the desert, the men in the pickups parked on the highway were there much earlier, arriving while even the great white house itself was barely visible. They sat and drank coffee and smoked. One or two remarked that the cowboys were already up.

"Hell, I always said that it would take the Second Coming to get them up by dawn on a Sunday," an old rancher said and cackled. The joke spread from truck to truck until the whole caravan was laughing about it.

Just as the sun broke the surface of the hills, casting a rib of sun onto the peak of Billings's house, a figure in white appeared on the roofline, eased along the catwalk, and stood on the observation platform looking off toward the village.

"That's him, that's him!" Like a jolt of electricity the word spread from truck to truck. The cowboys on the steps of the bunkhouse saw too and stood, though they, like most of the men on the road, had seen him many times on the roof at dusk. This was different—almost, as Nathan Warwick put it as he stood with his fellow cowboys by the bunkhouse steps, a religious moment: the stark white figure against the brightening sky ready to descend and walk across the desert to his people, in his hands the Gospel they must live by.

Bob Billings, if it was Bob Billings in the robe that day, disappeared into the house, reappeared at the back door, and walked off toward the Mexican village. The men in the trucks sat silently and watched, along with the cowboys before the bunkhouse, as he shrank to a white dot at the edge of the hills, then vanished into them. When he disappeared, the caravan, now joined by three other trucks from town and the cowboys in another pickup, headed off to Nuevo Cielo, just over twenty miles by road, to await his emergence on the other side.

He never came out. The Mexicans, lined up in expectation outside their church, stood in eager silence looking off to the north as the morning sun mounted to noon and the desert hills became one vast shimmer. The men from town sat in their trucks talking quietly among themselves, drinking beer and smoking and waiting.

God never returned to Nuevo Cielo. Some said that the men who managed the family fortune grew displeased with the way Billings had plowed money into the village and sent out their footmen in the long black cars to abduct and murder him, while others argued that it was Mexican farmers who felt they had lived beneath this blasphemous human god too long who slew him in the desert and buried his body. Still others believed that Mexican bandits killed him for the money they thought he might have in the box, while some contended that Billings left the country and is living even now on an exotic island somewhere in a corner of the world where he is God to other dark people. No evidence of foul play was ever discovered, though baffled townspeople scoured the hills for days, some using metal detectors to search the sand for Billings's brace.

Sheets of the Gospel were found hither and thither in the desert over the next year or two, blown from the boot box that the sheriff from Divot discovered on a rock in the hills the afternoon of Billings's disappearance. Pieces of the handwritten lined paper may still be found in curiosity shops as far away as Dallas, selling as slivers of the ark might, and in a display case in the library in Divot, guarded rigorously by a sharp-eyed curator, is a quarter-inch-thick portion of the manuscript, beside it a piece of white cloth that a young cowboy declared he found not a mile from the box a week after the disappearance.

* * *

The houses of Nuevo Cielo are shacks again, the green grass gone, the waterworks a wreck, and the church has been stripped to a shell of concrete blocks and tin. Only a few old farmers remain to work with their families small vegetable patches at the edge of the encroaching sand. They work, they wait, and daily they look toward the hills to the north for the God in white who will come to deliver them once again into the world of plenty. The cowboys, those remaining on the dying Double Star, sit evenings on the bunkhouse steps and watch the outline of the great house, not so much believing that a white figure will emerge against the sky as hoping that it might and fearing that they will not be there when it does.

ABOUT THE AUTHOR

A native Mississippian, Paul Ruffin is the author of three poetry collections and editor or co-editor of several anthologies, the most recent of which is *That's What I Like (About the South) and Other New Southern Stories for the Nineties*. His fiction has appeared in many literary magazines and anthologies including *Southern Review, Ploughshares,* and *Best of the West*. He teaches English at Sam Houston State University in Huntsville, Texas, where he edits *The Texas Review*.